Samuel French Acting Edition

The Christmas Carol

by Brian Way

SAMUEL FRENCH

SAMUELFRENCH.COM   SAMUELFRENCH.CO.UK

FOR PRODUCTION ENQUIRIES

UNITED STATES AND CANADA
Info@SamuelFrench.com
1-866-598-8449

UNITED KINGDOM AND EUROPE
Plays@SamuelFrench.co.uk
020-7255-4302

Each title is subject to availability from Samuel French, depending upon country of performance. Please be aware that *THE CHRISTMAS CAROL* may not be licensed by Samuel French in your territory. Professional and amateur producers should contact the nearest Samuel French office or licensing partner to verify availability.

MUSIC USE NOTE

Licensees are solely responsible for obtaining formal written permission from copyright owners to use copyrighted music in the performance of this play and are strongly cautioned to do so. If no such permission is obtained by the licensee, then the licensee must use only original music that the licensee owns and controls. Licensees are solely responsible and liable for all music clearances and shall indemnify the copyright owners of the play(s) and their licensing agent, Samuel French, against any costs, expenses, losses and liabilities arising from the use of music by licensees. Please contact the appropriate music licensing authority in your territory for the rights to any incidental music.

IMPORTANT BILLING AND CREDIT REQUIREMENTS

If you have obtained performance rights to this title, please refer to your licensing agreement for important billing and credit requirements.

<u>THE CHRISTMAS CAROL</u>

In the Distance a Church Bell chimes the hour, others join in, many others, growing nearer and nearer to us, until all are dominated by one bell which is quite close.

With the bells, light slowly fades to the sombre gloom of a smoky and foggy London Street ....but the gloom is in sharp contrast to the hearts of people. We hear laughter, we hear a voice call "A Merry Christmas" and others answer, and there is more laughter. And we hear carol-singers approaching nearer, nearer, nearer, until they are actually with us, standing under their lanterns, solemnly and yet lustily singing out their hearts.

Other people pass them in the street, some hurrying with holly and Mistletoe and Christmas trees, others, laden with baskets of good christmas food or gift-parcels, are glad to linger and rest their burdens for a moment, and there is a crippled beggerman, who simply enjoys the gaiety and the company. These are people coming and going on their way home. It is cold - and all these people are cold on their extremeties: cold on their noses and the tips of their fingers: and their feet are cold. But they also feel the warmth and gaiety and hope of Christmas, and it is this feeling they share, each with another, even with complete strangers. And we hear the sound of coppers in the collecting tins of the carol singers - and the singing itself is freely punctuated with the simplest words: "Thank you, sir." "Merry Christmas to you." "And to you." And so on.

But now another man comes very forcibly to the carol-singers. He stands for a moment, too angry to speak, quite unnoticed by the singers, but avoided by one or two other passers-by. Even the cripple moves a little farther away - and suddenly SCROOGE gives vent to his anger.

SCROOGE   Silence this wretched caterwauling.

But the singers sing.

SCROOGE   Silence, I say.

And the singing dies away.

SCROOGE   How can a man work against such noise?

There is silence now, and glances from one to another, and a smile, and a bold voice calls out "A merry Christmas, Mr Scrooge," and others add their greeting.

SCROOGE   Humbug.

A youngeman in the group - Scrooge's nephew, FRED   comes forward....

FRED
(To his companions) Let me speak to him. *(To SCROOGE)* A Merry Christmas, Uncle.

SCROOGE
Who calls me uncle?

FRED
Who else but your nephew?

He laughs disarmingly and others laugh with him, enjoying both the joke and the courage behind it.

SCROOGE
Huh! Fred! I might have known.   Wasting your time, caterwauling with others as lazy as yourself.

FRED
Caterwauling, perhaps.   But not wasting time.

A VOICE
Why not join us, Mr Scrooge?

ANOTHER
Yes, come and sing with us.

ANOTHER
We could do with a deep, deep bass.

And there is laughter again and preparations to start another carol.   Through it another voice is loud and clear.

VOICE
And what about Bob Cratchit?   He can sing with the best of us.

FRED
Good idea, I'll fetch him.

SCROOGE
No, sir, you shall not fetch him.

FRED
No, uncle?   Then I'll call him. *(Calling - joined quickly by others.)* Bob.   Bob Cratchit.

And there is more Gaiety and bustle and excitement as they call.   And as Bob Cratchit comes out there are cheers and greetings and hasty explanations.   And the joy is cut by Scrooge with a single word.

SCROOGE
Cratchit!

There is silence.

SCROOGE
Cratchit, return to your work.

CRATCHIT
But - but, sir.....

SCROOGE
Don't "But, sir," me, Cratchit.   Return to your work.   This instant.

FRED   Come, uncle, be kind....

SCROOGE   Kind, sir? I pay my clerk fifteen shillings a week. I doubt he's worth it, but I pay it. I pay it every week and I expect him to work every week.

FRED   But uncle, it's Christmas.

SCROOGE   Christmas. Humbug.

FRED   Christmas a humbug. Come, you don't mean that.

SCROOGE   I do mean it. Merry Christmas! What right have you to be merry? What reason have you to be merry? You're poor enough.

FRED   Then what right you you to be miserable? What reason to be morose? You're rich enough.

SCROOGE   Bah! Humbug!

He attempts to leave them, but FRED cuts him off.

FRED   Don't be cross, uncle.

SCROOGE   What else can I be when I live in such a world of fools as this? Merry Christmas! Out Upon Merry Christmas!

And as he goes on he speaks not only to FRED but to others in the group - buttonholing them, penetrating the warmth of their goodwill with the frozeness of his own misery.

        What's Christmas time to you but a time for paying bills without money? A time for finding yourself a year older and not an hour richer? A time for balancing your books and finding every item in 'em dead against you? If I could work my will, every idiot who goes about with "A Merry Christmas" on his lips should be boiled with his own pudding and buried with a stake of holly through his heart. He should.

FRED   Uncle!

And others join in with simple protests.

SCROOGE   Nephew! Keep Christmas in your own way, and let me keep it in mine.

FRED   Keep it! But you don't keep it.

SCROOGE   Let me leave it alone, then.   Much good may it do
                 you!   Much good it has ever done you!

FRED   Oh, uncle, really.   There are lots of things that
                 I'm sure have done me - good, as you call it, without
                 me making a penny from them, Christmas among the
                 rest.

*There is agreement with what he says, and other moments of
agreement as he goes on.*

                 But, surely, Christmas - well, Christmas is
                 different.....

SCROOGE   Different?

FRED   Yes.   I've always thought of Christmas as a good time.

SCROOGE   A good time!

FRED   Yes, a good time.   Oh, I know what you're thinking -
                 you're thinking I mean a - a lazy, good-for-nothing
                 time.   But I don't mean that.   I mean a good time -
                 a time when you, when you feel good, when you make an
                 effort, a real effort, to be pleasant and kind - and
                 forgiving - and charitable.   No uncle, you listen to
                 me.   It's the one time in the year when you open up -
                 open up your heart; and - and you notice other
                 people; doesn't matter what they're like - you
                 realise they're alive, they're flesh and blood, they
                 love and hate, and sing and laugh, and cry and suffer ·
                 yes, uncle, suffer.   Just on this one day a year -
                 one day - that's all, just one day, we have a thought
                 for them as well as ourselves.   And that's what
                 Christmas means to me, uncle - just that.   It may
                 never have put a penny in my pocket, but I believe
                 that it has done me good, and will do me good - and I
                 say God bless it.

*There is a moment's silence - then BOB CRATCHIT, who has
been listening in the background, comes forward a little
clapping.   SCROOGE turns to him.*

SCROOGE   Let me hear another sound out of you, and you'll keep
                 Christmas by losing your job.   *(To Fred.)* You're
                 quite a powerful speaker, sir.   I wonder you don't
                 go into parliament.

FRED   Uncle, don't be angry.   Come, dine with us tomorrow.
                 Come and spend Christmas with me and my wife and ....

SCROOGE   I'll see you in hell first.

FRED   But why?   Why?

SCROOGE   Why did you get married?

FRED   Why?   Because I fell in love.

SCROOGE   Because you fell in love.   Good afternoon.

FRED   Oh, come, uncle.   You never came to see me before I
            got married, so why give it as a reason for not
            coming now.

SCROOGE   *(Again trying to move away.)*   Good afternoon.

FRED   I want nothing from you.   I ask nothing of you.   Why
            can't we be friends?

SCROOGE   Good afternoon.

FRED   I'm sorry, uncle.   Heaven knows I've tried.   What
            else can I say?   What else can I do?

SCROOGE   You can move out of my way.   And you can take your
            friends off somewhere where their singing won't
            disturb my work.

FRED   Very well, uncle.   But just let me remind you of
            this.   We've never yet had a quarrel that's been my
            fault - and we never will.   Certainly not on Christ-
            mas Eve.   And if you change your mind - you'll still
            be welcome.

SCROOGE   Good Afternoon.

FRED   *(Laughing)* Not just good afternoon, uncle.   But - A
            Merry Christmas.

SCROOGE   Good Afternoon.

FRED   And a Happy New Year.

SCROOGE   Good afternoon.

*But now all join Fred in calling "A Merry Christmas" and "A
Happy New Year" - and then FRED starts them all on "God Rest
Ye Merry Gentlemen, Let Nothing You Dismay" and as they sing
they start to go.*

*SCROOGE returns to his office and to his books .... he is
followed in my an anxious BOB CRATCHIT, who creeps to his
own desk and lights a candle to work by ....*

SCROOGE   You're another of them.   A clerk earning fifteen
                 shillings a week......thinking you have a right to
                 a merry Christmas....I'll retire to Bedlem.   Get
                 on with your work.

BOB   Yes, sir.   I'm sorry, sir.

                 *SCROOGE at once starts adding up rows and columns of
                 figures.....Cratchit too tries to work.....but he is too
                 cold....he goes to the fire and pokes it about...but nearly
                 puts it out and has to blow on the ashes to try to keep it
                 alive...then he attempts to creep past SCROOGE to get some
                 coal...*

SCROOGE   Cratchit!   Coal is an expensive commodity.   I work
                 out to a penny exactly what we need and when we need
                 it.   Get on with your work.

BOB   It seems to be particularly cold today, sir.

SCROOGE   Then get on with your work.   There's nothing like
                 work for getting a man's mind off things like the
                 weather.

BOB   Just one shovel full, please, sir.

SCROOGE   No, Cratchit.   We have used all the coal we need
                 for today.   Don't let me have to tell you again -
                 get on with your work.

BOB   Yes, sir.

                 *BOB sits down, frozen - and pathetically tries to warm
                 himself over the light of the candle...and SCROOGE
                 continues to add his figures...getting very worried.*

SCROOGE   Cratchit.

BOB   Yes, sir.

SCROOGE   Come here, Cratchit.

BOB   Yes, sir.

SCROOGE   Cratchit - three times I have checked the Petty Cash
                 total for this week.

BOB   Yes, sir, I left the details on your desk... it came
                 to six shillings and eightpence, sir.

SCROOGE   It comes to five shillings and eightpence, Cratchit.
                 I tell you I have checked it three times.

BOB	Yes, sir, but the coal and the candles sir account for....
SCROOGE	There are no receipts for coal and candles, Cratchit. Furthermore, I did not authorise the expenditure of an additional shilling on coal and candles.
BOB	Well, there was none left, sir.
SCROOGE	Of course there was none left. You waste them.
BOB	Certainly there were no candles....
SCROOGE·	I am not interested in your candles. Use daylight, Cratchit. You light the candles too soon. Daylight is cheaper. Do you understand.
BOB	Well, sir, I.....
SCROOGE	Do you understand?
BOB	Yes, sir. But....
SCROOGE	I am glad you understand, Cratchit. I shall deduct the shilling from your salary so that the accounts will in no way be inconvenienced. That will be all, Cratchit.
BOB	But, sir. please.
SCROOGE	That will be all, Cratchit. Fetch me the Book of Debtors.
BOB	Yes, sir.

BOB goes miserably for the book and Scrooge continues to add and check his columns of figures.

BOB returns with the book....

SCROOGE	*(Looking up a particular entry.)* Ah, yes, I thought as much. His debt should have been paid yesterday. Was it?
BOB	No sir.
SCROOGE	*(After a pause.)* Continue, Cratchit.
BOB	Well, sir the people came, but ...
SCROOGE	And when did they come?
BOB	When you were at the Exchange, sir.

SCROOGE   You asked them to wait.

BOB   They couldn't wait, sir.

SCROOGE   So why didn't you take their money and give them a
                 receipt. I've told you often enough.

BOB   Well sir.....

SCROOGE   Why?

BOB   Sir - they hadn't got any money, so I couldn't take
                 it.

He is unable to go on....

SCROOGE   Well?   Well?

BOB   Well, sir, they said they would be able to pay next
                 week and I said - well, I said that I was sure you
                 would understand, sir.

SCROOGE   You said what? Well? *(BOB is too afraid to speak.)*
                 I shall take out a summons at once, Cratchit.   If
                 people do not pay their debts then they must go to
                 prison for it, and their goods must be confiscated...

BOB   Oh, they will pay, sir.   I'm sure of that.

SCROOGE   You're sure of that!   And do not interrupt me.   Do
                 you suppose I should be where I am now if I had the
                 same attitude as yours, Cratchit?

BOB   They will pay, sir.   They just need a little more
                 time.

SCROOGE   And they shall get a little more time, Cratchit. In
                 the debtors prison.

BOB   But, sir, it's Christmas.

SCROOGE   Christmas - humbug! What has Christmas to do with it?
                 Get back to your work Cratchit before you ruin me.

BOB   Yes, sir.

And CRATCHIT goes back to his work..

*Two portly gentlemen arrive, very business-like, fussing with
papers.   They see BOB CRATCHIT first.*

1st GENT   Is this - is this Scrooge and Morleys?   *(CRATCHIT
                 indicates SCROOGE.)*   Ah, thank you, yes.   Yes. *(They
                 move to SCROOGE.)*

1st GENT   Have I the pleasure of addressing Mr Scrooge or
Mr Morley?

SCROOGE   Mr Morley has been dead these seven years.   He died
seven years ago this very night.

1st GENT   Well - we have no doubt his generosity is - is, er -
continued by yourself, sir.

*He hands SCROOGE his credentials. SCROOGE looks at them
briefly and hands them back.*

SCROOGE   Good afternoon.

2nd GENT   Mr Scrooge.   At this festive time of the year,
Mr Scrooge, it is more than usually desirable that we
should make some slight provision for the poor and
destitute; as you no doubt realise, they suffer
greatly at the present time, Mr Scrooge.

1st GENT   Indeed, indeed.   Thousands of people lack even the
ordinary necessities of life, let alone the simplest
of comforts.   We therefore feel that...

SCROOGE   Are there no prisons?

1ST GENT   Plenty of prisons.

SCROOGE   And the Union Workhouses?   Are they still in operation?

1st GENT   They are, sir.   I wish I could say they were not.

SCROOGE   The Treadmill and the Poor Law are in full vigour
then?

1st GENT   Both very busy, sir.

SCROOGE   Oh!   I was afraid that from what you first said that
something had occured to stop their useful work.   I
am very glad to hear it.

2nd GENT   But Mr Scrooge, neither the prisons nor the workhouses
provide exactly what you or I - or for that matter any
other human being - would call Christmas Cheer.

1st GENT   Precisely.   So, Mr Scrooge, a few of us are raising
a fund to provide the poor with meat and drink and
means of warmth.   What shall I put you down for?

SCROOGE   Nothing.

1st GENT   Er - you mean you wish us to withhold your name?

SCROOGE   I wish to be left alone.   Since you ask me what I
                 wish gentlemen, that is my answer.   I don't make
                 merry myself at Christmas, and I can't afford to
                 make other people merry - particularly idle people.
                 I help to support both the prisons and the workhouses -
                 and they cost quite enough.   Idle people who are
                 badly off must go to them.

2nd GENT   Many can't go to them.

1st GENT   And many would rather die.

SCROOGE   Then let them die - and decrease the surplus
                 population.   It is none of my business.

2nd GENT   Sir - it is the business of all of us.

SCROOGE   No, sir, not all.   If you consider it your business,
                 then you had better attend to it, and allow me to
                 attend to mine.   Mine occupies me constantly.   Good
                 afternoon, gentlemen.

*For a moment the SECOND GENTLEMAN, though non-plussed, seems
to want to continue: but the FIRST GENTLEMAN pulls him away.
CRATCHIT would like to run forward, to give them something,
but under the eye of SCROOGE he dare not do so.   And as the
TWO MEN leave, the clocks strike the half-hour, and CRATCHIT
is at once alert.*

SCROOGE   Time to go home, I suppose.

CRATCHIT   Well - er - yes, sir.

SCROOGE   Yes, sir!   And you consider you've done an
                 afternoon's work?

CRATCHIT   Well, there has been rather a lot of excitement,
                 sir.   But - then, we expect it at Christmas, don't
                 we, sir?

SCROOGE   You expect it, Cratchit.   I - ignore it.   At least I
                 do my honest best not to let it interfere with my work.

CRATCHIT   Yes, sir.

SCROOGE   And I suppose you'll want the whole day off for
                 Christmas tomorrow.

CRATCHIT   Well, if its quite convenient, sir.

SCROOGE   It's not convenient - and it's not fair.   If I was
                 to stop half-a-crown from your wages for it, you'd

think yourself ill-used, I'll be bound!   Yet you don't think me ill-used for paying a day's wages for no work.

CRATCHIT   It is only once a year, sir.

SCROOGE   Only once a year.   A poor excuse for picking a man's pocket every twenty-fifth of December.   However - I suppose you must have it.

CRATCHIT   Thank you, sir.

SCROOGE   Be here all the earlier next morning.

CRATCHIT   Yes sir.   Thank you sir.   Merry Christmas, sir.

SCROOGE   Out upon a merry Christmas.   Humbug, I say.   Humbug.

And so violent is he with these words that CRATCHIT is glad to be off home as fast as possible.   SCROOGE starts on his journey home.   A longish journey during which he talks a great deal to himself...

SCROOGE   Curse the fog.   And curse the stupity of the whole world.   Christmas! Humbug!   It's nothing but stealing.   Calling it charity doesn't change it from what it is.   Stealing. And listen to them... the bells, the singing, the laughter...pretence.   That's what it is.   Nothing but pretence, *(The lone voice of a small BOY is heard singing a carol.   SCROOGE angrily shouts him away.   The BOY laughs and runs.)* Instead of getting down to work and solving their problems through honest labour they pretend all is well and hide behind the laughter and the singing... and they expect everybody else to do the same.   Well, at least old Jacob Marley and I avoided any such nonsense.   We lived frugally, we worked hard.   No man owed us anything and we owed nothing ourselves. *(He stops for a moment thinking of JACOB.)*   Poor Jacob.   Seven years ago this very night.   You were a good man of business Jacob.   Ah, but the business hasn't suffered by your going... *(He stumbles..)* Curse the fog and the darkness.   Never mind.   A house stuck away in the darkest alley is a good investment...the rooms are good to let for business and there's still enough space for living..Ah, where is that door?   I can feel it with the knocker...

He stares at the knocker.

What's this?   What's this?   What am I seeing? *(He is staring at the knocker.)*   No, Jacob.   No.   Whatever else it could do your face could never serve as a

knocker on a door.   Jacob, don't haunt me like
this..... I won't believe it.   I won't. I won't.

*And in his terror he crashes the knocker and the vision goes.
There are hideous echoes throughout the house of the door
noise.*

There.   There.   Just a moment of fancy.   It means
nothing, nothing at all....

*And yet as he goes through the door he instinctively looks
back to see if there is anything behind the door...*

Nothing - at all. What did I expect?   To see his
pigtail hanging on the other side. Humbug.   It's
all humbug!

*He fastens the door...and goes on up the stairs towards his
room...*

Jacob you chose well when you chose a staircase as
wide as this.   You could drive a coach and four up it
in comfort....aaahhh...

*For a moment he is again frightened by some sound or imaginary
sight.*

Humbug!   There's nothing to be afraid of.   The
offices are empty...the wine cellar below is empty...
and there's enough light through the window from the
street lamps to save having any other light...

*He arrives at the top and goes to his own room...But the
sights and sounds have unnerved him a bit, and he readily
checks that there is nothing concealed anywhere.*

Nobody under the table. Nobody under the sofa.
Nobody under the bed. Nobody in the cupboards or the
closet.. nobody inside my dressing gown. Humbug.. of
course there's nobody.   What on earth have I to fear?
It's all fancy.   Nothing but fancy.   I'll just take
a good pot of gruel this one...lasted all the week.

*He puts the gruel on to the embers of the fire and starts to
undress...*

Too cold to undress fully on a night like this. And
no need anyway with a good thick dressing gown...a
dressing gown to last for years. Has lasted for years,
and'll see my life out yet. What? What?

*And again he hears some sound and crosses to his door and
looks, quite motionless to check that there is nothing there...*

Humbug....nothing but humbug....

And he goes to eat his gruel...All the time he is eating there are some signs and portents of all not being well. He hears faint footsteps in the distance...He hears a coach drive up and stop outside and waits fearfully...doors creek and slam..but still nothing particular happens in his own room...

Then a single door bell rings..his own..and then other bells in the house, picking up a great and terrifying cacophony of sounds..which suddenly cut out...and there is the single sound of the approach of the GHOST OF JACOB MARLEY. (Author's note: this sound, in Dicken's terms, is made by a long chain of keys and cash boxes and other symbols of the avariciousness of the two men; in production, such a chain can lead to laughter and might be more atmospherically replaced with a single chain and the dragging of feet.)

THE GHOST which in one sense fills SCROOGE with terror, and in another does no more than challenge his disbelief, slowly approaches - and then stops a little way from SCROOGE....

SCROOGE
What do you want with me?

MARLEY
Much.

SCROOGE
Who are you?

MARLEY
Ask me who I was.

SCROOGE
You're mighty particular for a ghost. Who were you then?

MARLEY
In life, I was your partner, Jacob Marley.

SCROOGE
Yes. Yes, so you seem. Can you sit down?

MARLEY
I can.

SCROOGE
Do it then. You look more exhausted than you did seven years ago.

MARLEY
(Sitting, after a moment.) You don't believe in me?

SCROOGE
No, I don't.

MARLEY
What proof can I offer you, beyond that of your own senses?

SCROOGE
I - I don't know.

MARLEY
Why do you doubt your senses?

SCROOGE	Because - well, because a little thing can affect them, a slight disorder of the stomach makes them cheats. You may be a bit of undigested beef - or a blot of mustard - or a crumb of cheese - or even a bit of an underdone potato. There's more of gravy than of grave about you, whatever you are. You see this toothpick?
MARLEY	I do.
SCROOGE	You're not looking at it.
MARLEY	But I see it, all the same.
SCROOGE	Well, I have but to swallow this to be tormented for the rest of my days by a whole legion of ghosts. Humbug, I tell you. Humbug.

At this, MARLEY sets up a terrible cry, which frightens SCROOGE so much that he falls on his knees....

SCROOGE	Mercy. Mercy. Why do you trouble me?
MARLEY	Do you believe in me or not?
SCROOGE	I do. I must. But tell me, Jacob - why do you walk the earth? And why do you trouble me?
MARLEY	Listen, and I will tell you.
SCROOGE	Yes, yes, tell me, Jacob, tell me. Tell me.
MARLEY	Listen! Be still - and listen.

SCROOGE'S cringing and whining subsides.

MARLEY	It is required of every man that the spirit within him should walk abroad among his fellow-men, and travel far and wide; and any spirit that does not do so during life is condemned to do so after death - is condemned to wander through the world, as I am now, Ebenezer Scrooge; as I have been these seven years. As you have said, I am exhausted with restless wandering over seven whole years.
SCROOGE	But the chains, Jacob? The chains. Why.....
MARLEY	I forged them myself.
SCROOGE	You?
MARLEY	They are a heavy and a painful burden - and yet I made them myself during my own wretched life. The

                              chains you are forging, Ebenezer, will be no less
                              heavy   You are forging them yourself, link by link.

SCROOGE   No, Jacob. No. Speak comfort to me, Jacob.

MARLEY   I have none to give. Comfort comes from other Spirits,
                              Ebenezer - and is given to other kinds of men.   My
                              spirit never moved beyond our counting house - and
                              weary journies lie before me...

SCROOGE   But you were always a good man of business, Jacob.

MARLEY   Business! Mankind was my business. The common
                              welfare was my business. Charity, mercy, kindness
                              were all my business. Making money was only a drop
                              in the great ocean of my business. Why did I walk
                              through crowds of fellow-beings with my eyes turned
                              down, and never raise them to that blessed star which
                              led the wise men to the poorest stable? Why? Why?

                    And as if in answer to his question the church clocks peel
                    again.

MARLEY   Hear me. My time is nearly gone.

SCROOGE   I will, I will. But don't be hard upon me; don't
                              be flowery, Jacob, please.

MARLEY   How it is that I appear before you in a shape that you
                              can see, I may not tell. I have sat beside you
                              many, many times - invisible.

SCROOGE   No, Jacob, no.

MARLEY   Tonight I am here to warn you - to warn you that you
                              have yet a chance and hope of escaping my fate; a
                              chance and hope of my making, Ebenezer.

SCROOGE   You were always a good friend to me.   Thank 'ee.

MARLEY   You will be haunted by three spirits.

SCROOGE   Is - is that the hope and chance you mentioned, Jacob?

MARLEY   It is.

SCROOGE   I - I think I'd rather not.

MARLEY   Without their visits, you cannot hope to escape the
                              path I tread. Expect the first tomorrow, when the
                              bell tolls one.

SCROOGE   Couldn't I take 'em all at once and have it over,
                 Jacob?

MARLEY   Expect the second on the next night at the same hour.
                 The third upon the next when the last stroke of
                 twelve has ceased to sound.   Do not expect to see me
                 again.   But - for your own sake - remember what has
                 passed between us.   Remember.   Remember.

*And as he speaks, the GHOST OF JACOB MARLEY slowly backsaway
from SCROOGE, and then disappears altogether.*

*For a moment SCROOGE seeks after him. He manages to get out
the word "Humbug" but without conviction.   Then, tired and
troubled, he goes to bed, clothed as he is...and sleeps.*

*There is silence and stillness..silence and stillness.. and
and awesome feeling of expectancy..SCROOGE sleeps. (Note: If
it is intended to use anything in the way of a real bed, it
is to the point that Scrooge slept in a four-poster, with
the four curtains fully drawn.)*

*During his sleep he is restless with a terrible nightmare.
Suddenly the clock strikes the quarter.. and at once SCROOGE
is awake..*

SCROOGE   A quarter past!

Again the clock strikes.

SCROOGE   Half past!

Again the clock strikes.

SCROOGE   A quarter to it!

And again the clock strikes.

SCROOGE   The hour itself!   And nothing else!

*But before his relief can take root, the clock strikes one.
Immediately there is more light..and the light is moving
towards SCROOGE, revealing to him the SPIRIT OF CHRISTMAS
PAST.*

*(Note: Dickens' own description of this ghost is well worth
studying, but possibly very difficult to carry out in some
respects, particularly that of "from the crown of its head
there sprang a bright clear jet of light..with a great
extinguisher for a cap, which is not held under its arm.."
The author would suggest that simplicity be the absolute
key-note of this ghost, with fully considered contrast with
the others.   The final ghost, the GHOST OF CHRISTMAS YET
TO COME, needs to be in a dark cowled, full-length robe, for
the face is never visible; the second, the GHOST OF
CHRISTMAS PRESENT, needs to be bright and gay...it is therefore*

*suggested that this first apparition be in a full white
tunic, of a simple nature, without any attempt to do "the
bright clear jet of light from the head"..and yet, at the
same time, to follow Dicken's thoughts of "Its hair, which
hung about its neck and down its back, was white, as if
with age; and yet the face had not a wrinkle in it, and
the tenderest bloom was on the skin..it wore a tunic of the
purest white; and round its waist was bound a lustrous
belt, the sheen of which was beautiful." Possibly also -
"It held a branch of fresh green holly in its hand; and, in
singular contradiction of that wintry emblem, had its dress
trimmed with summer flowers.")*

THE SPIRIT stops, quite close to SCROOGE.

SCROOGE	Are - are you the spirit, sir, whose coming was foretold me?
C. PAST	I am.
SCROOGE	Who and what are you?
C. PAST	I am the Ghost of Christmas Past.
SCROOGE	Long past?
C. PAST	No. Your past.
SCROOGE	Well - what business brings you here?
C. PAST	Your welfare.
SCROOGE	Very nice of you, I'm sure. But don't you think an uninterrupted night's sleep might do me even more good?
C. PAST	Come! Rise - and walk with me. Come!

SCROOGE shrinks from this idea.

SCROOGE	But where will you take me?
C. PAST	To see mysteries you've forgotten.
SCROOGE	Mysteries!
C. PAST	Moments from your past - your own past.
SCROOGE	I - I - er -
C. PAST	Are you afraid?
SCROOGE	No, but I - I -

C. PAST   Let me touch you but once, and you will find there is
                 nothing to fear.

THE SPIRIT moves towards him, its hand outstretched.

SCROOGE   Keep away from me.   No, no.   Keep away.   Don't
                 touch me.   Don't...

C. PAST   But once...

*SCROOGE is too afraid to move.   THE SPIRIT reaches out and
touches him over the heart...*

C. PAST   There!   Now you will find there is nothing to fear.

SCROOGE   *(Discovering just that, despite himself)* - No.   No.

C. PAST   Follow me.

*Sounds come...and SCROOGE follows THE SPIRIT.   And as they
journey the light and the air change...and time too.   After
a while, SCROOGE stretches out his hand and touches THE
SPIRIT...*

SCROOGE   Spirit, wait!   Wait!   *(THE SPIRIT stops; but does
                 not speak.)*   I - I know this place.

C. PAST   You remember?

SCROOGE   I lived here as a boy.   I could walk it blind fold.

C. PAST   Strange to have forgotten it for so many years.   Look.
                 Look.

*And as SCROOGE looks he sees a strange kaleidoscope of
shadowy forms moving in front of him. And there are voices on
the air, calling Christmas and New Year wishes to each
other.*

SCROOGE   I know them.   I remember each and every face.   I
                 remember them from all those years ago..no..don't go.
                 Stay...stay with me...

*But the shadows fade, and SCROOGE is again alone with THE
SPIRIT.*

C. PAST   Your lip is trembling.   And what is that on your
                 cheek?

SCROOGE   *(Wiping away the tear.)*   It's, it's a pimple.

C. PAST   You remember - and I think you understand - you feel
                 the past.

SCROOGE   Quickly, spirity - take me where you will.   I'll
                           follow.

C. PAST   Come.

Again they journey...and again the light and the air change ..
And the SPIRIT suddenly stops.

C. PAST   Look.

SCROOGE looks and sees the shadow of a child sitting alone.

SCROOGE   It's a child.

C. PAST   What child?

SCROOGE   It's me, Spirit - alone, at school - waiting. Waiting.

C. PAST   Were you often alone?

SCROOGE   Nearly always, Spirit, I had no friends at school.
                           My father hated me so I was seldom at home. I tried
                           at school - I think I tried.   But I had no friends
                           to speak of.   *(A TEACHER enters to THE BOY - looks*
                           at him, hands him a book.)   My real friends - my
                           only friends - were those in books, Ali Baba -
                           Robinson Crusoe - Robin Hood - They were my friends.

C. PAST   Look!   *(A fantasy sequence bringing these to life*
                           for the lonely boy.)

Again for a moment there is the shadow but this time THE
SHADOW soon becomes substance.

C. PAST   Remember?

SCROOGE   I - I think I remember.

C. PAST   You last day at school.   Look - your sister Fan.

And as SCROOGE looks, he sees himself on the day of leaving
school, pacing about the room, again waiting..and very soon
FAN comes to him.

FAN   I have come to bring you home.

SCROOGE   Home?

FAN   Yes, home home - for ever and ever.

SCROOGE   But - father?

FAN   Father's agreed.   Oh, you won't even know father;
             he's so changed, so kind.   So -

SCROOGE   But why? - what's happened?

FAN   Who knows what's happened. Just suddenly - one night -
             he spoke so gently to me when I was going to bed that
             I thought I'll ask him now - just this once more -
             whether you could come home!   And he said "Yes; yes,
             you should come home.   And he's arranged the coach
             for me to fetch you.   And he's arranged that you
             don't have to come back here any more.   And he's
             arranged that we shall all be together for Christmas -
             and that we shall have the merriest time in all the
             world.

SCROOGE   Oh, Fan, how wonderful.   How wonderful.

FAN   Quickly, now. The coach is waiting.

SCROOGE   Not so fast, little Fan, not so fast.

FAN   But we mustn't waste a minute.

SCROOGE   I must fetch my books and - and -

FAN   Quickly then, fetch it. Fetch it.

SCROOGE   Now wait.   I must stop being so excited.   I can't
             even think properly.   *(Very still for a moment.)* Fan,
             it's too wonderful.   Say it again: I'm going home -
             and I don't have to come back here ever again.   You
             did say that, didn't you?   I didn't dream it.

             Before FAN can answer a loud voice calls from off:

SCHOOLMASTER   Bring down Master Scrooge's box, there - and see it
               loaded on to the coach.

             *And the SCHOOLMASTER comes to FAN and SCROOGE THE YOUNGER.
             He is carrying a decanter of wine and three glasses on a
             tray.   SCROOGE is both fearful and embarrassed by the loud-
             ness and the condescension of this SCHOOLMASTER, who stops
             suddenly.*

SCHOOLMASTER   Master Scrooge!   I suppose we'll have to get used to
               Mister Scrooge from now on, eh? We're a man, now,
               aren't we, boy?

SCROOGE   Well, yes, sir, I - I.

SCHOOLMASTER   I've seen many change from Master to Mister in my time.

Not an easy change to make, boy.   It's a new life;
new responsibilities;   new endeavours, and this young
lady, I take it, is your sister.

SCROOGE   Yes, sir, my sister, Fan.

SCHOOLMASTER   *(Pouring wine for the three and passing the glasses.)*
I don't approve of young people drinking in the normal
way - as you, boy, might well remember.   However,
this is a special occasion.   I give you a toast - to
Christmas, and to - Mister Scrooge!   May you treat
the world as it's treated you here.

*They drink.   Then FAN moves quickly to SCROOGE, her
excitement in no way quelled by the SCHOOLMASTER.   She raises
her glass to him.*

FAN   To Mister Scrooge.

*And light fades from them and back to the GHOST OF CHRISTMAS
PAST and SCROOGE THE ELDER.*

C. PAST   Your sister was always frail.   But she had a great
heart.

SCROOGE   Yes, she had.   You're right, spirit, she had.

C. PAST   She died when still a very young woman;   a married
woman, with children.

SCROOGE   One child.   Only one.

C. PAST   True.   Your nephew.

SCROOGE   Yes.   My nephew - Fred.

Pause.

C. PAST   Come - let us see another Christmas.

*And again there is a change of light as they journey a little
way. And again THE GHOST stops.*

C. PAST   Look.   Do you remember this place?

SCROOGE   Remember it?   Why - I was apprenticed here.   Dick and
I.

D. PAST   You remember Dick?

SCROOGE   Dick was my greatest friend.   We did everything
together. And we were apprenticed to dear old
Fezziwig, bless him.

C. PAST   Dear Fezziwig.   Look.

And OLD FEZZIWIG comes in "laughing all over himself, from his shoes to his organ of benevolence."

FEZZIWIG   Yo ho, there! Ebenezer! Dick!

SCROOGE, now a young apprentice, and DICK WILKINS run in.

FEZZIWIG   Yo ho, my boys.   No more work tonight. Christmas
                         Eve, Dick.   Christmas, Ebenezer. We've got one
                         minute, my boys, to make the place fit for a party;
                         one minute before the guests arrive!

DICK & SCROOGE   Yes, Mr Fezziwig.

The preparations are fast and furiously gay.   A table is brought in and gayly decorated with food and drink and candles. A tree, perhaps, and other forms of decoration. The Fezziwig ball is a matter of production and improvisation.   The preparation merges into the festivities themselves. People arrive quickly on top of each other.

FIRST - The Fiddler, who tunes up his instrument like
*   "fifty stomach-aches."*
THEN - Mrs Fezziwig and
*   - One of her simpering daughters,*
*   - One of the daughter's eager pursuers, who for most*
*   of the party rivals the attentions of Dick Wilkins.*
THEN - Belle, to whom Ebenezer is at once devoted.

(Author's note: this completes the whole cast for the party as it is essential that Scrooge the elder and the Ghost of Christmas Past watch the proceedings.)

MR FEZZIWIG is a constant bustle of jovial hospitality, making sure that all have something to eat and drink from the moment they arrive.   The scene includes -

1) The above arrival, greeting, eating and drinking;

2) A short, fast dance involving everybody;

3) A game of blind man's buff, in which Ebenezer is the one blind-folded. He catches Belle, and his prize, to everyone's delight - is a kiss - sweeping us into

4) Another gay dance, but there are moments of greater individuality in these:

- Ebenezer and Belle, then
- Mr and Mrs Fezziwig, then
- The Fezziwig girl, turn and turn
*   about with Dick and his rival,*
* Then for a moment again*
- Ebenezer and Belle.
- And then everybody at their
* wildest delight again.*

(Author's note: There is no suggestion in Dickens that Belle was at this dance; however, by bringing her in at this stage, and focussing some definite moments on her growing relationship with Ebenezer, will undoubtedly help the next scene and add an essence of continuity that is rather essential at this stage.)

Throughout the whole scene, SCROOGE THE ELDER is elated almost to the point of being pulled into the scene himself; and as this dance ends, light begins to fade from the scene with everyone wishing everyone a Merry Christmas and a great many "thank-you's" to MR FEZZIWIG for having such a wonderful party. SCROOGE and BELLE predominate in these thanks. And as the scene fades altogether, we concentrate again on SCROOGE and THE GHOST OF CHRISTMAS PAST: SCROOGE, momentarily is still filled with glee.

SCROOGE   Dear old Fezziwig.   Dear old Fezziwig....

And as the last light of the scene fades, and OLD FEZZIWIG's laugh fades, SCROOGE becomes aware of the GHOST, and subsides.

C. PAST   A small matter - to make these silly folk so happy and so full of thanks.

SCROOGE   Small!

C. PAST   Is it not? He spent but a few pounds - three or four at the most.   Is that so much to deserve such praise?

SCROOGE   *(Still with some of the excitement he has just experienced.)* It isn't that, Spirit, it isn't that. He had the power to make us happy or unhappy.

C. PAST   Us? Who do you mean?

SCROOGE   All of us.   But mainly Dick and I; we worked for him, we were his apprentices.   He had the power to make our work light or heavy, a pleasure or a dreadful burden; and he used that power.   He used that power; he used it in hundreds of little ways - in the way he spoke to us, or looked at us or asked us to do things.   That's the kind of happiness he gave to us - and you can't buy that, even with a fortune.   You - you can't....

Suddenly he realises THE GHOST is staring at him and he stops.

C. PAST   What is the matter?

SCROOGE   Nothing in particular.

C. PAST   Something, I think.

SCROOGE   No, nothing. I just wish, at this moment, I could
                   say a word or two to my clerk, Bob Cratchit. That's
                   all.

THE GHOST watches him for a moment, then breaks the mood.

C. PAST   My time grows short. Quickly. Let us see another
                   Christmas.

*Again light changes as they journey a little way. The
light reveals to us SCROOGE, still young, but slightly older
than in the last scene. He is fully mature. The gaiety of
the Fezziwig evening has left him, in its place is a driving,
self-centred, eager ambition. And we see him now, with
books, checking details, adding figures, excited and gripped
by a world of business and commerce.*

*(This factor is of tremendous importance as quite clearly
Scrooge, deep within himself, could have been quite different
from the way he turned out; but the great determination to
"better himself" and to "safeguard the future" became an
obsession, until all the normal and everyday delights and
struggles of living were superseded by a singular determination to make money. As Belle puts it; "The Golden Idol
supersedes all;" in more modern terms, Aspiration is
superseded by Ambition.)*

SCROOGE   No, no, Spirit, don't show me this. Spare me this.

C. PAST   You remember the place?

SCROOGE   I remember.

C. PAST   You remember the occasion?

SCROOGE   How could I ever forget? It was a moment concerning
                   a particular opportunity.

C. PAST   Two particular opportunities. This moment might be
                   called the cross-roads in your life. You had to
                   choose.

SCROOGE   I chose as best I could. I thought I was doing the
                   right thing. My whole future depended on it.

C. PAST   Your whole future. What of others? What of their
                   future?

SCROOGE   Their future was their own affair. It was nothing to
                   do with me.

C. PAST   Look again - and see.

SCROOGE   No, spirit, no.

C. PAST   Look, I say.

And SCROOGE looks, and sees other people come to his former self: Belle, with whom he danced and to whom he is now engaged; Dick, his fellow apprentice and friend; Dick's Girl.

DICK   Come on, old man. If we don't go now we shall miss all the daylight. My feet are just tingling with the thought of a skate.

SCROOGE looks up for a moment, but is deeply involved in figures and continues to check them.

DICK   *(With a mixture of mock and genuine impatience.)* Ebenezer!

THE GIRL   Oh, he's all wrapped up in another of his silly old books. Come on, Ebenezer.

DICK   We'll soon move that. Come, Ebenezer, the books'll keep till tomorrow. For today - it's skating and then supper. *(Playfully snatching the books away.)* Let's put the books to bed, shall we?

SCROOGE   Dick, don't do that.

DICK   But the books are fed up with work. And it's Christmas.

SCROOGE   Give them back....

DICK   Tomorrow morning.

SCROOGE   I said "Give them back".

DICK   Ooooooh, hoity-toity, and at Christmas too.

SCROOGE   Give - them - back! Dick!

DICK   *(To his GIRL.)* Here, catch.

SCROOGE   *(laughing at DICK.)* Will you give that back to me at once, please.

DICK   *(Throwing the book to his GIRL.)* When you're a good boy and promise to forget all about them till tomorrow.

SCROOGE   Dick, will you stop fooling about and give me that book.

DICK   *(Just as SCROOGE lunges at his GIRL.)* **Look out.**

*The GIRL laughs as she throws the book back to DICK, and
for a few seconds they go on teasing SCROOGE in this way,
throwing the book backwards and forwards, taunting SCROOGE
with a kind of pig-in-the-middle-game.   And he gets more
and more angry.   And finally intercepts the book.*

SCROOGE   Now, leave it, will you.

DICK   *(Going to him again.)* **Aw, come, Ebenezer.**

SCROOGE   *(Really angry.)*   I said leave it.

And there is dead silence and stillness for several seconds.

DICK   Sorry.   I didn't realise you were serious.

SCROOGE   Well, I am.

DICK   But we arranged this party months ago.

DICK's GIRL   Months!   We arranged it last Christmas.

SCROOGE   All right, we arranged it a year ago.   Things can
                        change in a year.   I'm sorry, but I can't come.

DICK   *(Quite innocently incredulous.)* You what?

SCROOGE   I said I can't come.

*Now DICK and HIS GIRL are fully sensitive to the situation
in terms of BELLE, who all this time has said nothing, but
has just stared at SCROOGE.   At first thinking he was part
of the game that DICK was trying to play, and then
gradually realising the fuller truth.   Now... in the
silence, in the awareness that DICK and HIS GIRL have
played their full hand.. she speaks for the first time.*

BELLE   Happy Anniversary.

SCROOGE turns to her and looks at her, but cannot answer.

BELLE   Happy Anniversary, my dear.

SCROOGE   *(Still angry.)* Happy Anniversary!   Don't try to get
                        round me now with Happy Anniversary!   There's
                        always something!   Anniversaries, birthdays,
                        Christmas.   Always something!   It's nothing but
                        Humbug.   Humbug, humbug, humbug.....

DICK
All right, then it's humbug, whatever that may mean.
But just get one thing straight, Ebenezer - I'm
through after this.   Do you understand.   I've
tried and I've tried and I've tried - God alone
knows how I've tried - well I'm not trying any more.
It's up to you now.   Understand?

SCROOGE
Please yourself.

DICK
I said d'you understand.

SCROOGE
Oh, do as you like, only leave me alone.

DICK
(Controlling himself for a long pause.) All right.
I will leave you alone. *(To his GIRL.)* Come on.

As they reach the door, he turns to BELLE.

Belle?

BELLE
I'll come in a moment.

DICK
We'll wait for you. *(Pause.)* I'm sorry, Belle.

*He waits only long enough for BELLE to smile her
reassurance and then goes, followed by HIS GIRL.   There is
silence between SCROOGE and BELLE.   BELLE breaks it.*

BELLE
Ebenezer, dear...don't you think...don't you feel
that....that...

SCROOGE
That he's right?   Is that what you're going to say?
That Dick's right? *(BELLE tries to interrupt but
SCROOGE takes no notice.)* If you think he's right
Belle, then you must do what you think's best.   I
won't interfere.   Only don't expect me to give up
everything I've worked for just for the sake of some
damn-fool skating party that you know as well as I
do will be as boring as the last one, and doesn't do
anything for any of us.

BELLE
I wasn't going to say that.

SCROOGE
If that's the kind of life you want then you're
welcome to it, only you'd better find someone else
to give it to you, 'cos I wont.

BELLE
You don't really care about us at all, do you?

SCROOGE
Oh, don't be petty?

BELLE

You don't, do you?   Oh, you did once, I know.
Four years ago when we became engaged, but its
gradually dwindled away until now it hardly exists
at all.

SCROOGE

For heavens sake Belle, don't start all that...

BELLE

The only thing you really care about now is money.
Money, money, money.

SCROOGE

Business is a man's life.   There's no place for
women.

BELLE

Exactly, and there's no place for women in such a
life.   Very well, Ebenezer.   You have your world
of business and I hope you enjoy it.   And I hope
your money will bring you all the comfort you need
right through your old age.

SCROOGE

Can't you begin to understand that...

BELLE

Yes, I understand completely.   I understand that
I'm in your way and that the only thing that will
ever matter to you is making money. Well, there - take
it.   I'll never stand in the way of your ambition.

*And she throws her ring - the engagement ring he gave her -
on the ground and leaves him.   He looks at it.   Turns it
over with his foot, then moves angrily away from it.*

SCROOGE

Humbug.   Parties and Christmas and the whole wretched
lot of it.   Nothing but humbug.

*And as the YOUNG SCROOGE goes on muttering humbug, light
fades from the scene and back to the SPIRIT and SCROOGE.*

SPIRIT

That was the turning point, wasn't it?   Nothing but
humbug.

SCROOGE

Please, Spirit, take me away from here.

SPIRIT

No.   You shall see again each Christmas that
followed.   The whole miserable growth of that
terrible world of humbug.

*And there follows a fast-moving almost nightmare sequence
of Christmas upon Christmas of the world of SCROOGE and
business.   The world in which everything that was not
strictly business was nothing but humbug.*

*The sequence is fast moving.   With many people coming and
going.   All in a rather brittle and stylised manner.   A
real nightmare.*

1st VOICE   Please sign this, Mr Scrooge.

2nd VOICE   The market is in your favour, Mr Scrooge.

3rd VOICE   Buy now, Mr Scrooge.   Buy as much as you can.

1st VOICE   Your signature will confirm the deal, Mr Scrooge.

2nd VOICE   Sell now, and you'll make a fortune, Mr Scrooge.

BIG BUSINESS MAN   You're doing well, Mr Scrooge. Don't worry about
                           your future - it's quite secure with us.

4th VOICE   Sign here, Mr Scrooge.

2nd VOICE   Profits are up again, Mr Scrooge. Up by seventy-
                           five per cent.

1st VOICE   Profits still rising, Mr Scrooge. A better year even
                           than last.

BIG B. MAN   There's promotion ahead for your kind, Scrooge. We're
                           making you manager.

2nd VOICE   Sell, now, sir, and you'll double your profit.

3rd VOICE   Your feeling for the market is amazing, Sir.

1st VOICE   Just sign, sir, that's all.

BIG B. MAN   Mr Scrooge, my colleagues and I have discussed your
                           future. We have decided to ask you to join the
                           Board of Directors.

SCROOGE   You're a little late.

BIG B. MAN   Late?

SCROOGE   I'm setting up in business on my own - in partnership
                           with Jacob Marley.

BIG B. MAN   What?

SCROOGE   If I were you I'd anticipate losing most of your
                           business to us.   I doubt you'll see the year through.
                           Just a warning.

And the sequence now involves JACOB MARLEY as well.   And
the two of them make more and more money.

2nd VOICE   Profits are up again, gentleman.

1st VOICE	Just sign here, sir.
3rd VOICE	Sign here, please.
2nd VOICE	Profits are up a hundred per cent on the last quarter.

And a YOUNG MAN comes to them about a debt.

YOUNG MAN	But, Mr Scrooge, I don't think I can pay back all of the fifty pounds in so short a time.
SCROOGE	That's your affair. However, I must warn you. The longer the time the greater the interest.
YOUNG MAN	And if I can't pay it back?
SCROOGE	Then you shall go to prison.
YOUNG MAN	But, sir, I have a wife and three children.
SCROOGE	And I, sir, have a business to run. Good afternoon.
YOUNG MAN	I beg of you, sir, for the sake of Christmas.
SCROOGE	Christmas! Humbug!

As the YOUNG MAN goes, SCROOGE turns to JACOB MARLEY.

SCROOGE	A good year, Jacob. A good year.
JACOB	A very good year, Ebenezer. A merry christmas to us both.
SCROOGE	Humbug.
JACOB	Yes, humbug. But we can wish ourselves a Prosperous New Year.

And back comes the BIG BUSINESS MAN.

BIG B. MAN	I appeal to you, gentlemen. At the rate you are going you will put us out of business altogether.
JACOB	Really. How unfortunate.
SCROOGE	I did warn you.
BIG B. MAN	What do you expect me to do, then?
JACOB	Sell out to us. What else?
SCROOGE	At our terms.

And the MAN goes away, unable to do anything.

SCROOGE	We need a clerk, Jacob. Pity. It's a waste of money.
JACOB	Have you anyone in mind?
SCROOGE	Just the man, I think.

And BOB CRATCHIT comes to them

BOB	Thank you, gentlemen.
SCROOGE	Wages - fifteen shillings a week.
BOB	And prospects, sir.
SCROOGE	Hard work.
JACOB	And the chance of a permanent position if you prove yourself worthy of it.
SCROOGE	At the same wages, naturally.

And now the action is even faster, with CRATCHIT feverishly trying to keep pace with the books of figures. Much of this is unspoken while the following dialogue continues.

1st VOICE	Sign here, gentlemen.
2nd VOICE	We bought out three more firms today, sir.
BOB	More people owe us money this year than ever before.
SCROOGE	And the interest?
BOB	Double last years.
SCROOGE	Not enough.
JACOB	But things are improving, Ebenezer.

A YOUNG MAN comes to them.

YOUNG MAN	I can't possibly pay this week, gentlemen.
JACOB	Then we shall send you to prison.
YOUNG MAN	Couldn't I have a little more time?
SCROOGE	Much more time - in prison.
YOUNG MAN	But, gentlemen....
SCROOGE	Good afternoon.

COLLECTOR   Could you make a small gift to this very special
                   charity, sir.

JACOB   No, we couldn't.   Leave us alone.   We're busy.

COLLECTOR   But. Sir...

SCROOGE   We're busy.   Good afternoon.

*During the next moment, JACOB MARLEY crumbles up and is
tended by BOB CRATCHIT.*

CHARITY MAN   Sir, our organisation looks after the sick and needy.

SCROOGE   Then you had better look after your organisation.

CHARITY MAN   With your help, I will, sir.

SCROOGE   Do I ask you to look after mine?

CHARITY MAN   No, sir, but...

SCROOGE   Then don't ask me to look after yours.

CHARITY MAN   But, sir, the sick - and the dying.

SCROOGE   Good afternoon.

As the MAN goes BOB comes quickly to him.

BOB   Please, sir, I think Mr Marley is ill.

SCROOGE   Get back to your work, Cratchit.

BOB   But, sir, I think he's really bad.   He may even be
                   dying.   Surely there's something we can do.

SCROOGE   Yes, Cratchit, there is.   We can work twice as hard.
                   The fortunes of Scrooge and Marley cannot be lost
                   simply because Mr Marley is ill.

*Now SCROOGE starts adding up figures in the background, his
words continually audible during the following sequence.*

*"One hundred, a hundred and fifty, two hundred, two fifty,
three hundred..." and so on, by fifties, to however many
thousands or hundreds of thousands he might reach during
the action.*

The action is as follows:
*BOB CRATCHIT nurses JACOB, he fetches a blanket and tries to
make him warm and comfortable.   He smoothes his brow, now
and again he turns and looks appealingly for help to SCROOGE.*

who takes no notice, finally, with some heavy gasps, JACOB raises himself a little and falls back dead. BOB covers him with the blanket. Other men come and take MARLEY's body away. SCROOGE looks up as they go. A bell tolls...

BOB   Isn't it dreadful sir.   And on Christmas Eve, too.

SCROOGE   Christmas Eve.   Humbug. Humbug, I say.

BOB looks his contempt at SCROOGE and then turns disgustedly away.

SCROOGE   Cratchit.   Although I am now the only partner in the firm, we shall leave the name as "Scrooge and Marley" - it will be better for business.

And light swiftly fades from the scene to THE GHOST OF CHRISTMAS PRESENT and SCROOGE.

SCROOGE   Take me away from this place.

PAST   I told you that these were shadows of things that happened in the past. That they are what they are is nothing to do with me.

SCROOGE   I cannot bear any more. Take me home. Take me home.

PAST   I will take you home. But - learn from what you have seen.

SCROOGE   I will, Spirit. At least - I will try.

PAST   Come, follow me.

And as SCROOGE follows, light fades and so ends Act 1.

ACT 2

SCROOGE is again asleep.   All is silent.

*(Author's note: Everything should be done to avoid comedy
at the beginning of this act; Dickens makes reference to
Scrooge awakening in the "middle of a prodigiously tough
snore" - which could start the whole act on an entirely wrong
note.   Within Scrooge himself, there is now a growing
awareness of the necessity to accept all the visitors
promised by Jacob Marley - but the arrogance and the defiance
are fully on the wane, replaced as much by fear as by any
other emotion; the seeds of simple, straightforward humility
have already been sown - ultimately from these will grow hope.*

*SCROOGE wakes before the bell strikes, and lies waiting for
it, knowing that it is coming, and when it does come, ready
not to be surprised by any form the spirit might take. But
as the bell strikes, all that happens is that he is brightly
lit by a strange ruddy light...nothing else, no apparition,
and this being the one thing he is not ready for, he is
filled with an even greater fear. He waits and watches for
a long time, but still there is no apparition. Then he
senses that the ghost and the light must in some way be
connected, and, feeling the presence of the ghost somewhere
else, leaves his bed and begins to move towards it...and
suddenly he sees the figure silhouetted against the light.*

*(Author's note: Possibly the high rostrum over the main
entrance could be used for this ghost, with the light on
Scrooge coming from behind it.   However, whatever way is
used in production, the important point is that this GHOST
does not, like the first and the last, COME TO SCROOGE, but
that Scrooge, by his own will and intention, GOES TO THE
GHOST, despite his terror....)*

*As SCROOGE approaches the GHOST, light suddenly changes, brigh
lighting up the GHOST OF CHRISTMAS PRESENT.*

*(Authors note: Again Dickens description of the ghost is
worth considering, though in carrying it out, simplicity
should again be the key-note; he describes him as "a
jolly giant, glorious to see...bearing a glowing torch, in
shape not unlike Plenty's horn...clothed in one simple
deep green robe, or mantle, bordered with white fur..the
garment hangs loosely so that the breast is bare...the feet
also are bare.... on its head no other covering than a
holly wreath, set here and there with shining icicles..its
dark brown curls are long and free...girded round its middle
is an antique scabbard, but with no sword in it..and the
ancient sheath is eaten up with rust.*

C. PRESENT   Come in; come in, and know me better, man.

*SCROOGE goes timidly a little closer to him, awed and filled
with wonder by all he sees. But despite THE GHOST'S warmth
and friendliness and geniality, he is unable to look at him,
partly because of all that surrounds him.*

C. PRESENT   I am the Ghost of Christmas Present.   Look upon me.
                    Look upon me.   You have never seen the like of me
                    before.

SCROOGE   I have never seen so wondrous a spread of Christmas
                    cheer.   So many turkeys and geese; so much game
                    and poultry and brawn; such great joints of meat,
                    and suckling pigs, and such wreaths of sausages.

C. PRESENT   Ahh, but look here to this side, look at these.

SCROOGE   So many Christmas puddings - and such large ones.
                    And mincepies, and red-hot chestnuts, beautiful red
                    apples, and juicy oranges and luscious pears, and -
                    fruit of every kind.

C. PRESENT   And still that is not all.   Look - look over there.

SCROOGE   Cakes, the most wonderful Christmas cakes - and sweets -
                    and nuts and raisins - and yet more sweets - and
                    more sweets -

C. PRESENT   And over here...

SCROOGE   Seething bowls of punch - and ginger wine - and; oh,
                    no Spirit, I have never seen the like of any of this
                    before.

C. PRESENT   Have you not met any of my brothers?

SCROOGE   Your brothers?

C. PRESENT   I am the Spirit of <u>this</u> Christmas.   Last year was
                    the turn of one of my brothers - the year before that
                    of another - the year before that another - and so on,
                    back through time.

SCROOGE   Then you have had many brothers?

C. PRESENT   More than eighteen hundred.

SCROOGE   A tremendous family to provide for.

*Suddenly for a moment, the joy seems to leave THE SPIRIT,
and he towers almost menacingly over SCROOGE, searching for
the meaning and the attitude behind these words...SCROOGE
continues hurridly...*

SCROOGE   Spirit, take me where you will. Last night I was
                 compelled to look on the shadows of the Past.
                 Tonight, if you have anything to teach me, let me
                 profit by it.

C. PRESENT   Touch my robe.

But SCROOGE is afraid to do so.

C. PRESENT   Touch my robe.

SCROOGE   Where shall we be going, Spirit?

C. PRESENT   Among our fellow men.

SCROOGE   But where? In the streets?

C. PRESENT   In the streets.   In people's homes...

SCROOGE   Whose homes?

C. PRESENT   You shall see.

SCROOGE   Yes, I shall see.   But - I am afraid to <u>be</u> seen.

PAUSE.

C. PRESENT   You shall not be seen, as I am not seen.   But as
                 the Spirit of Christmas Present, I have only a short
                 while to live, and much work to do.   You shall come
                 with me and see that work.   You shall see people in
                 every walk of life.

SCROOGE   People I know?

C. PRESENT   Some you will know.   Others you will not even have
                 thought of.   People in the remotest parts of the
                 world...people across the seas and on the seas....
                 people of good fortune and people who suffer.

SCROOGE   How can you visit so many?

C. PRESENT   Because I am a Spirit.

SCROOGE   But do all these people know of your visit?   Even
                 though they cannot see you?

C. PRESENT   Some know - without the need to see me.   Others
                 would not know even if they did see.   But I visit
                 them all, those who reject me as well as those who
                 welcome and accept me. *(He holds his torch high.)*
                 To each and every one I give something from the light
                 of my torch.

And as he holds it up high, the light brightens.

G. PRESENT   Are you ready?

SCROOGE   Yes, Spirit, I am ready.

G. PRESENT   Then touch my robe - and we shall be invisable.

SCROOGE fearfully touches the robe. Immediately the lights change and we are in the streets of London on Christmas eve. TWO ERRAND BOYS, laden with goods, come from either end of the street. They collide with each other, scattering their goods.

1st E. BOY   Why don't you look where you're going?

2nd E. BOY   Me!   It wasn't my fault.

1st E. BOY   Course it was.

2nd E. BOY   You clumsy oaf.   I'll box your ears.

1st E. BOY   Come on, then.   Settle it now.

And by now SCROOGE and THE GHOST are close to THE BOYS, and THE GHOST sheds the light from his torch on them...

2nd E. BOY   *(Putting down his fists.)* - Ah, I shall be late if I do.

1st E. BOY   So shall I.   Anyway, I'm sorry. Maybe it was partly my fault.

2nd E. BOY   No, you're not to blame.   I was hurrying too much. Here, let me help.

And they start to help each other with their goods.

1st E. BOY   Cor, you've got some good grub there.   Where you taking it then?

2nd E. BOY   Up to the Big House.

1st E. BOY   Are you? I've just been up there.   Gave me a tanner they did.

2nd E. BOY   Did they? I'd better hurry.

1st E. BOY   See you for skating?

2nd E. BOY   Yes, I'm going soon as shop's shut.

1st E. BOY   Sorry to bang into you.

2nd E. BOY	Me too.

And they go on their way - and THE SPIRIT smiles at SCROOGE. No sooner have they gone than TWO ELDERLY PEOPLE come down the road.

1st E.P.	Oh, I can't go another step. My whole body aches, fit to drop, it does.
2nd E.P.	But you can't give up now. Keep trying. That's it. Keep trying...
1st E.P.	I can't tell you. I simply can't.
2nd E.P.	But you must.
1st E.P.	I haven't the strength.

And the SPIRIT raises his torch over them...

2nd E.P.	Come on, now. One last effort, eh. T'isn't too far.
1st E.P.	All right, bless you. Just for the sake of Christmas.
2nd E.P.	That's it. That's lovely. I knew you could do it.

And as they wander on, another PERSON comes quickly past them, ignoring them...the PERSON is laden with parcels. Before he can get to the corner, the SPIRIT raises his torch. The PERSON stops and turns, and goes back to the ELDERLY COUPLE.

PERSON	Can I be of any assistance?
2nd E.P.	No, no, really, thank you. We can manage perfectly well. We've not far to go now.
PERSON	Are you sure?
1st E.P.	Quite sure, thank you. It's very nice of you to ask.
PERSON	Well, happy Christmas to you.
1st E.P.	And to you. Thank you for asking.
2nd E.P.	Happy Christmas and a Merry New Year.
PERSON	Thank you.

And the PERSON goes on his way...

1st E.P.	Now, wasn't that thoughtful.
2nd E.P.	It's like I always say. There's something about Christmas. Sort of does something to people. That's it. You're doing beautifully now. **Nearly there.**

And they go from our sight down the street.

SCROOGE	*(To SPIRIT.)* Does your torch always work such wonders?
C. PRESENT	Not always. Look.

A THIEF stealthily makes his way down the street and pauses to look over his shoulder. THE SPIRIT sheds the light of his torch. THE THIEF spits and goes on about his business.

C. PRESENT	You see - it is rejected by some.

The lights begin to change.

C. PRESENT	We shall see Christmas in the home of your clerk, Bob Cratchit.
SCROOGE	No, Spirit, I would rather not see that.
C. PRESENT	"If you have anything to teach me, let me profit by it". They were your own words. The Cratchits have much need of the light from my torch.
SCROOGE	Then - show me. Show me.

The GHOST raises his torch. The lights change again, and we are in the Cratchit home.

The people in the scene are:

> *Bob Cratchit*
> *Mrs Cratchit, his wife*
> *Martha Cratchit (their eldest daughter)*
> *Belinda Cratchit (younger daughter*
> *Peter Cratchit (elder son)*
> *Tiny Tim (younger son, a cripple, who uses a crutch*
> *and has an iron frame on one leg.)*

All is hustle and bustle in the house, under the general supervision and guidance of MRS CRATCHIT.

MRS CRATCHIT	Belinda, keep an eye on the pudding, dear.
BELINDA	*(Coming in.)* It's a beautiful pudding, mother. Simply beautiful.

MRS CRATCHIT   Well, it won't be if we don't keep an eye on it.

MARTHA   *(Coming in.)* I'll lay the table, mother.

MRS CRATCHIT   Would you dear. Thank you. Oh, but could you get
                      the punch ready as well, Father's sure to want us
                      to have a toast before dinner.

MARTHA   He's done it himself.

MRS CRATCHIT   Then let's put it on the fire in here and keep it
                      warm.

MARTHA   I'll fetch it.

MRS CRATCHIT   What's Peter doing?

PETER   *(Coming in.)* I'm doing the potatoes. Look at
                      them, mother. They're the best I've ever done them.
                      And they taste delicious.

MRS CRATCHIT   Yes, and you taste much more of them and there won't
                      be any left.

PETER   I only had a little.

MARTHA   *(Coming back.) Oooooo. (She stands still in the
                      middle of the room.)*

PETER   What's the matter with you?

BELINDA   Just smell that goose.   There never was such a
                      goose.

MRS CRATCHIT   Listen!   Here's your father back from church with
                      Tiny Tim.

PETER   Quickly, Martha, hide.   Hide.

BELINDA   Yes, do, do.   Quickly.

MRS CRATCHIT   You better hurry or he'll catch you.

MARTHA   All look the other way or something.

          *MARTHA hides.   EVERYBODY ELSE looks quite innocent, and
          BOB CRATCHIT arrives with TINY TIM on his shoulder. TINY
          TIME is carrying his crutch.*

BOB   Hello, all of you.   I hope we're in time.

          He sees the gloomy faces.

BOB	Why, what's the matter? Where's our Martha?
MRS CRATCHIT	She's not coming.
BOB	Not coming!
MRS CRATCHIT	No, they've kept her at work.
BOB	Kept her at work! Not coming on Christmas Day!

But MARTHA can't keep it up any longer and comes from hiding.

TINY TIM	There she is! There she is!
MARTHA	Oh, father. I couldn't keep it up. I simply couldn't.
PETER	You've spoiled it.
BOB	You really had me worried.
MRS CRATCHIT	It's a shame to tease him on Christmas Day.
BELINDA	I want to show Tiny Tim the pudding.
TINY TIM	Please, please.
PETER	And the goose.
TINY TIM	Everything. I want to see all of it.
PETER	Come on then.

And he and BELINDA help the excited TINY TIM out to the kitchen.

MARTHA	I'll see they don't eat it all.

And she follows them.

BOB	My, it smells good.
MRS CRATCHIT	I hope it is Robert. And I hope there's enough.
BOB	Of course there'll be enough. You always worry about that.
MRS CRATCHIT	I'm sorry. I didn't mean...
BOB	No, I know you didn't. I never cease to marvel how you make a few shillings go so far.
MRS CRATCHIT	How did little Tim behave at church? Was he good?

BOB   Good as gold.   Even better.   But...

He stops and goes over to the punch.

MRS CRATCHIT   Tell me.

BOB   Well, he comes out with the strangest ideas.   He's
               a funny lad.

MRS CRATCHIT   What did he say?

BOB   I suppose it's sitting on his own so much.   He gets
               kind of thoughtful and then comes out with the oddest
               ideas you ever heard.

MRS CRATCHIT   He's doing all right, isn't he?

BOB   Oh, I think he's growing stronger, my dear.   I think
               so.

MRS CRATCHIT   Robert.

BOB   Anyway – he suddenly said that he hoped the people saw
               him in church because he was a cripple.

MRS CRATCHIT   What?

BOB   Yes, that's what he hoped.   He said that it might be
               pleasant for them to remember on Christmas Day who it
               was who made lame beggars walk and blind men see.
               Just like that.   Just as simple as that.

*For a moment they are silent.   Then the silence is broken by
by the return of the other members of the family, led by
TINY TIM.*

TINY TIM   It's a delicious pudding, mother.. and a great big
               goose. And, and, oh, it's all so wonderful.

BELINDA   If we don't eat soon, Peter will have finished all the
               potatoes.

PETER   Shan't.

MRS CRATCHIT   Is the goose done, Martha?

MARTHA   Beautifully done.   Just ready to eat.

MRS CRATCHIT   Then Robert?

BOB   Yes, my dear, we'll have a toast first.

PETER   Gosh, I forgot to look after the punch.

BOB   It's all right, Peter.   I've seen to it.

TINY TIM   Can I sit in my favourite corner for the toast?

MRS CRATCHIT   Of course you can.

BELINDA   *(Helping her father with the glasses and mugs as he pours out.)*   Here's yours mother.

BOB   And one for Martha.

PETER   I'll give Tiny Tim his.

BOB   There.   Have we all got some punch?

Choruses of delighted "yesses".

BOB   Then - A merry Christmas to us all, my dears.   God bless us.

And everybody re-echoes the toast.   Until finally...

TINY TIM   God bless us every one.

And THE SPIRIT holds them all for a moment in the glow of his torch, and the group freezes in the position of the toasting, light dims from them and comes up on SCROOGE and the SPIRIT.

SCROOGE   Spirit, tell me.   Will Tiny Tim live?

C. PRESENT   I see a vacant seat in the chimney corner.   I see a crutch without an owner.   If these shadows remain unaltered by the Future, the child will die.

SCROOGE   No, no, kind Spirit.

C. PRESENT   If these shadows remain unaltered by the Future, no other Spirit of Christmas will find him here.   But what of that?   If he's likely to die, then he'd better do it and decrease the surplus population.

SCROOGE   Don't, Spirit, don't...

C. PRESENT   Again, your words.   Man, don't use such words until you have discovered what the surplus is and where it is.   Will you decide what men shall live?   What men shall die?   It may well be that in the sight of Heaven you are more worthless, you are less fit to live than millions like this poor man's child.   What then?   What then?

SCROOGE turns away, crushed by the rebuke.

Listen.

The SPIRIT turns and again floods the CRATCHIT FAMILY with life and light, and SCROOGE turns as he hears his name.

BOB
Mr Scrooge!   I give you Mr Scrooge, the Founder of our Feast!

MRS CRATCHIT
The Founder of the Feast indeed!   I wish I had him here.   I'd give him a piece of my mind to feast upon!

BOB
My dear, please.   The children!   Christmas Day!

MRS CRATCHIT
Yes, and it needs be Christmas Day for one to drink the health of such an odious, stingy, hard, unfeeling man as Mr Scrooge.   You know he is, Robert!   Nobody knows it better than you do, poor man.

BOB
Please, please, my dear.   It's Christmas.

MRS CRATCHIT
I'll drink his health for your sake and for the sake of Christmas - but not for his.   Long life to him! A merry Christmas and a happy New Year.   He'll be merry and happy, I've no doubt.

And without much enthusiasm THE FAMILY drinks to "Mr Scrooge" and THE GHOST gives them the full warmth of his light for a moment, and as they burst again into good-hearted merriment and laughter, shaking away these last unhappy moments, he moves from them. And SCROOGE goes with him, backing away from the scene until it fades from sight altogether, and he and THE GHOST are alone again.

C. PRESENT
There is not time for you to see the lives of others in such detail.   We must move swiftly...

SCROOGE
Take me where you will, Spirit.   Show me what you will.   I'll follow - and gladly.

And as the lights fade dimmer and dimmer a howling storm rises up all around SCROOGE and the SPIRIT. And there is just the glimmer of a light visible through the storm.

SCROOGE
What place is this?   Why do we stand on this desolate moor in such a storm?

C. PRESENT
A miner's cottage.   The menfolk toil in the very bowels of the earth.   But they know me here, look.

And he brings a little more light to them with his torch. An OLD MAN and HIS WIFE and THEIR SON, and one of them sings an old Christmas song.   And the other two join in the

C. PRESENT   Come.   I must visit the lighthouse across the sea.

SCROOGE   Across the sea!   Spirit - We cannot cross the fury
                    of these seas.

C. PRESENT   Do not be afraid.   Follow me.

*And the howling of the storm is joined in force by the roar
of the sea. And then, through the darkness, close to hand,
they see the regular flashing of the light, and they move
nearer until they are within.   The TWO MEN who look after
the light raise their cans of grog to each other and shake
each other the warmest of Christmas greetings. And then one
of them sings a "sturdy" song, his voice rising above the
howl of the storm and the sea. And the SPIRIT sheds the
light from his torch on them both, then draws SCROOGE
slowly away.*

C. PRESENT   We shall see the light again very shortly, only next
                    time it will be from the deck of a fishing boat way
                    out at sea.   Come.

*And the lighthouse fades as they move away back into the
darkness of the storm. And soon they can just see the
lighthouse light, away in the distance, as they stand on the
storm-tossed deck of a small ship, pitching and tossing its
way through the storm.   Close to them is the shadowy figure
of THE SAILOR at the helm, soon he is joined by another who
brings him a mug of hot rum.   They can barely hear each
other as they shout above the fury of the storm.*

2nd SAILOR   Cap'n says we're clear south of the rocks.

HELMSMAN   What?

2nd SAILOR   The rocks.   We're clear south of 'em.

HELMSMAN   Thank God for the lighthouse.

2nd SAILOR   Aye.   Here's a find Christmas to 'em.

HELMSMAN   Aye. *(They drink.)* And to all of 'em safe in bed
                    at home.

2nd SAILOR   God bless 'em. *(Again they drink.)* And a happy
                    Christmas to 'ee, Tom.

HELMSMAN   Happy Christmas, Sam.

And again they drink, and THE SPIRIT shares the light of his torch with them, and the ship fades away. THE SPIRIT and SCROOGE are again alone.

C. PRESENT   Even in the dangers of the sea men do not forget me.

SCROOGE   Take me home, Spirit.

C. PRESENT   You said you would gladly follow.   Well?

SCROOGE   I'll try.   But away from these terrors.

C. PRESENT   Not home. But nearer home.   The home of your nephew - Fred.

No sooner said than done. There is suddenly bright light and tremendous roars of laughter, and THE SPIRIT and SCROOGE are in the midst of a party.

With: Fred, his nephew
*   Fred's wife*
*   His wife's pretty sister*
*   His wife's plain sister*
*   His friend, Topper*

FRED is the cause of the merriment, telling them a story.

FRED   He did.   As I'm alive, I swear he did.   He said Christmas was humbug. *(More laughter.)* And you know what's more?   He believed it, too.

Yet more laughter.

F'S WIFE   The more shame on him, Fred.

FRED   He's a comical fellow and that's the truth.

TOPPER   Comical!

FRED   Oh, he may not be all that pleasant, but he suffers more for it than we do.   At any rate, I've nothing to say against him.

F'S WIFE   I wonder how rich he is.

PLAIN SIS   Is he rich?

F'S WIFE   Fred says he is.

PRETTY SIS   He must be.

FRED   What of it? His wealth is no use to him. He doesn't do any good with it.   He doesn't make himself

comfortable with it.   And he certainly hasn't the
satisfaction of thinking he's ever going to benefit
US with it.

Again they all laugh.

F'S WIFE   I've no patience with him. *(There is general agreement.)*

FRED   Oh, I have.   I'm sorry for him.   I couldn't be
                   angry with him if I tried.   Well, who suffers by his
                   nasty whims?   Himself - nobody else.   Here he takes
                   it into his head to dislike us, and he won't come and
                   dine with us.   What's the consequence?   He doesn't
                   lose much of a dinner!

There are howls of protest and more laughter at this teasing.

F'S WIFE   Really, Fred!   I think he loses a very good dinner.

PRETTY SIS   So do I.

PLAIN SIS   A marvellous dinner.

FRED   Really?   Well, I'm delighted to hear it.   *(With a
                    wink at TOPPER.)*   Frankly I haven't too much faith
                    in these young cooks.   What do you say, Topper?

PRETTY SIS   If Topper's wise he won't say anything.

PLAIN SIS   Do stop teasing and go on with your story.

F'S WIFE   Fred never does finish a story.

TOPPER   I doubt he gets the chance.

More laughter from all.

FRED   I was only going to say that the consequence of dear
                    Uncle Ebenezer refusing to make merry with us is that
                    he loses some mighty pleasant moments that couldn't
                    possibly do him any harm - and he loses some
                    companions that couldn't help be pleasanter than those
                    in his own thoughts, whether he's in his mouldy old
                    office or his dusty old house.

F'S WIFE   But you won't ask him next year, will you?

FRED   I most certainly will.   I'll ask him every year.
                    Whether he likes it or not.

TOPPER   Why, when he always says no?

FRED	I pity him.
F'S WIFE	What a waste of pity.
FRED	Come, my dear, he's bound to change in the end.
F'S WIFE	Never.
FRED	Of course he will. If I go into his office every Christmas Eve for year after year, always in a good temper, always saying "A Merry Christmas, Uncle Scrooge, how are you?", eventually he's sure to say...
TOPPER	*(Acting the part.)* Humbug!

And again they all laugh.

FRED	You may all laugh - but something'll come out of it one day. You wait and see. And even if it only puts him in mind to leave his clerk fifty pounds - well, that's something.
F'S WIFE	Yes. Something we shan't live to see. Anyway, what a gloomy subject for Christmas. Just because he won't enjoy himself there's no reason why we shouldn't. What about a carol?

All agree, TOPPER suggests "Ding, Dong, Merrily on High," and THEY ALL sing lustily. (Audience participation.) SCROOGE watches with more and more excitement, and even joins in.

PRETTY SIS	Let's play "Yes and No".
FRED	Who's going to be asked the questions?
PLAIN SIS	Oh, you, Fred, please.
PRETTY SIS	He's marvellous at it. Please do, Fred.
FRED	All right. But give me half a minute to think of something.

There is excited anticipation as FRED thinks of something.

FRED	Right - I'm ready.
F'S WIFE	Is it animal?
FRED	Yes.
F'S WIFE	Alive?

FRED	Yes.
PRETTY SIS	Is it a nice animal?
FRED	No.
PLAIN SIS	Oh! A nasty animal?
FRED	Yes.
TOPPER	What sort of nasty animal?
FRED	Yes, no, yes, no, yes, no.

More laughter

PLAIN SIS	You can't ask questions like that. He's got to answer yes or no.
TOPPER	Sorry - er -
PLAIN SIS	Is it...
PRETTY SIS	No, give Topper a chance.
TOPPER	Is it a savage animal?
FRED	Yes.
PLAIN SIS	Oh! Does it growl?
FRED	Yes.
PRETTY SIS	Does it grunt?
FRED	Yes.
F'S WIFE	I know - it's a bear.
FRED	No.
F'S WIFE	Not a bear?
PLAIN SIS	A dog?
FRED	No.
TOPPER	Could we see this animal in London?
FRED	Yes.
TOPPER	In the streets?

FRED   Yes.

F'S WIFE   Is it some kind of circus animal?

FRED   No.

PRETTY SIS   Do people make a show of it?

FRED   No.

TOPPER   Do they lead it through the streets?

FRED   No.

F'S WIFE   Is it in a menagerie?

FRED   No.

TOPPER   Is it taken to market?

FRED   No.

PLAIN SIS   A circus animal?

PRETTY SIS   We've asked that once.

FRED   No.

PLAIN SIS   Sorry.

F's WIFE   Is it a horse?

FRED   No.

TOPPER   A donkey?

FRED   No.

PRETTY SIS   A goat?

FRED   No.

PLAIN SIS   A tiger

FRED   No.

TOPPER.   A bull?

FRED   No.

F'S WIFE   A cow?

FRED   No.

TOPPER   A pig?

FRED   No.

PLAIN SIS   Can it talk?

PRETTY SIS   Silly - it's an animal.

PLAIN SIS   Well, some animals talk.

FRED   Yes.

PLAIN SIS   It does talk?

FRED   Yes.

F'S WIFE   What? It growls and grunts - and talks?

FRED   Yes.

PLAIN SIS   I've got it.

PRETTY SIS   You can't have.

PLAIN SIS   I have, I have.   I know what it is, Fred.

FRED   what is it?

PLAIN SIS   It's your Uncle Scrooooge!

FRED   You're right.   Absolutely right.

There is great hilarity and congratulations.

F'S WIFE   You cheated, Fred.

FRED   I didn't cheat.

F'S WIFE   You did.   I said it was a bear and you said "No".
                You should have said "Yes".

*More laughter and banter and FRED hands them all some more
to drink.*

FRED   Listen everyone.   Whatever you may say about him.
                My old Uncle Scrooge has given us a great deal of
                merriment this evening.   It'd be ungrateful of us
                not to drink his health.   A Merry Christmas and a
                Happy New Year to the old man, whatever he is.   To
                Uncle Scrooge.

ALL   To Uncle Scrooge...

*And as they drink his health the light again fades away
from the scene, and there is again the sound of a bell
tolling.   The SPIRIT takes SCROOGE to see and hear other
people.*

C. PRESENT   Look - here.   The imprisoned...

*And faint light picks up a manacled prisoner. He is
staring into space and tapping his foot to the beat of some
tune that beats only in his own head.*

C. PRESENT   And here... The sick.

*And light cross fades to A SICK PERSON in bed, breathing
loudly in the same rhythm as THE PRISONER was tapping his
foot.*

C. PRESENT   And here - at these pathetic slaves, too starved
                       and hungry to work at all, but compelled by the
                       whip.

*And light cross fades to show TWO SLAVES, their feet
dragging in still the same rhythm, trying to carry heavy
loads, and when they falter, the whip keeps them going.*

C. PRESENT   And the blind...look, here...

*And light cross fades to a BLIND MAN tapping his stick in
still the same rhythm.*

C. PRESENT   And the lonely, the miserably lonely.

*And light again cross fades to show an old, OLD COUPLE,
sitting, too apathetic to do anything, except that one of
them sings a dreary and pathetic tune - still within the
same rhythm of hopelessness.*

*(N.B. with each of the above, the Spirit of Christmas
Present ages a little, both physically and in voice.*

C. PRESENT   And the very old, the forgotten...

*And light cross fades to show an old, OLD PERSON, energy
has died, will has floundered, and THE PERSON just rocks
backwards and forwards, backwards and forwards, soundlessly,
heedlessley, to the same rhythm of the tired and hopeless
heartbeat of spent life.*

*(N.B. Before turning from any person, the Spirit holds them,
for but a moment, in the glow of his torch, and each
person is by only the tiniest, subtle and almost
imperceptible fragment, helped a little...)*

*And as the final light fades and the bell ceases to toll,
THE SPIRIT OF CHRISTMAS PRESENT is also old, even though
he still has his vitality.*

SCROOGE
You - you have aged, Spirit.

C. PRESENT
My life upon this globe is very short.   These people
are now beyond even my help.

SCROOGE
What will happen to them?

C. PRESENT
That will depend on the actions of mankind.   I
have done all I can.

SCROOGE
When - when will your life end?

C. PRESENT
Tonight.   Tonight at midnight.   Hark!   The time is
drawing near.

*The clock bells chime the three-quarters after eleven...
All the time the bells are striking SCROOGE is staring at
THE SPIRIT's robe.*

SCROOGE
Spirit - forgive me for asking what my be none of my
business.   I saw someone, something - moving under
your robe.   Is it a foot or a claw?

C. PRESENT
It might as well be a claw for all the flesh there
is upon it.   Look here.

*And from his robe he throws forward TWO YOUNG PEOPLE -
wretched, abject, frightful, hideous and miserable for a
moment, they stand looking at SCROOGE who is transfixed
by the sight.   Then the two turn and throw themselves at
the feet of the SPIRIT, clinging to his robe.*

C. PRESENT
O Man, look at them.   Look down here.

*For a moment SCROOGE is too appalled to speak, then he
says...*

SCROOGE
Spirit - are they yours?

C. PRESENT
They are Man's.   And they cling to me, appealing
from their fathers.   This boy is Ignorance, this
girl is Want.   Beware them both, and all like them.
But most of all beware this boy, for on his brow I
see that written which is Doom, unless the writing
be erased.

SCROOGE
Spirit - have they no homes?

C. PRESENT
Are there no prisons?   Are there no workhouses?

*And the chimes strike midnight, and as they do so, light
drains away from the SPIRIT of CHRISTMAST PRESENT and his
two dreadful charges. And SCROOGE is left alone.*

*And on the final stroke of twelve SCROOGE sees, coming
towards him, A PHANTOM, completely shrouded in black, so
that the only visible part of it is one outstretched hand.
As THE PHANTOM reaches him it stops and remains absolutely
motionless, and SCROOGE kneels to it.*

SCROOGE   I am in the presence of the Ghost of Christmas yet
                           to Come.

*The SPIRIT does not answer, but remains motionless, with
outstretched hand.*

                           You are about to show me shadows of the things that
                           have not happened, but will happen in the time
                           before us? Is that not so, Spirit?

Still no answer.

                           Ghost of the Future, I fear you more than any spectre
                           I have seen. But as I know your purpose is to do me
                           good, and as I hope to be another man from what I was,
                           I am prepared to bear you company, and do it with a
                           thankful heart. Will you not speak to me?

No answer. But THE SPIRIT turns slightly, still pointing.

                           Lead on.   Lead on.   The night is waning fast, and
                           it is precious time to me, I know.   Lead on, Spirit.

*And THE SPIRIT takes SCROOGE into the streets.   There are
THREE BUSINESS MEN on the corner and THE SPIRIT stops so
that SCROOGE can hear their conversation.*

1st B.M.   No, no, no - I don't know much about it either way.
                           I only know he's dead.

2nd B.M.   When did he die?

1st B.M.   Last night, I believe.

3rd B.M.   Why, what was the matter with him?   I thought he'd
                           never die.

1st B.M.   *(Yawning.)* God knows.

2nd B.M.   What has he done with his money?

1st B.M.   I haven't heard.   Left it to his company, I imagine.
                           He hasn't left it to me.   That's all I know.

3rd B.M.   Well, it's likely to be a very cheap funeral; 'pon
             my life, I can't think of anybody who'd go to it.
             Suppose we make up a party ourselves?

1st B.M.   I don't mind - as long as lunch is provided. I
             must be fed if I go.

2nd B.M.   Well, I never go to funerals and I never eat lunch.
             But I'll offer to go, if anybody else will.   When
             I come to think of it, I'm not at all sure I wasn't
             the best friend he had - we used to stop and speak
             whenever we met.   Well, I must be off.   See you
             tomorrow.

1st B.M.   Bye, bye.

3rd B.M.   Bye bye.

*And they part company and leave, and THE SPIRIT takes
SCROOGE on a little way further. And again they stop as
two very wealthy and important BUSINESS MEN meet from
opposite directions, both of them in a great hurry.*

1st W.M.   Hello.   How are you?

2nd W.M.   Well, thank you.   And you?

1st W.M.   Fine, fine.   I hear old Scratch has got is own at
             last, eh?

2nd W.M.   So I'm told.   Cold, isn't it?

1st W.M.   Seasonable for Christmas-time.   You're not a
             skater, I suppose?

2nd W.M.   No, no.   Something else to think of. Good morning.

1st W.M.   Good morning.

*And they hastily part and go on their ways.   SCROOGE is
desperately puzzled, but before he has time to ask THE
SPIRIT any questions, they are passed by a filthy OLD HAG
with a large bundle.   She goes, and as she passes them, the
SPIRIT points and follows.   And SCROOGE growing more and
more curious, follows too.*

SCROOGE   **Where are we going, Spirit?**

*THE SPIRIT does not answer, simply stares at SCROOGE and
points the direction.*

SCROOGE   **Spirit - those men.   Who were they talking about?
             I knew some of them.   I met them nearly everyday at**

>   the Exchange.   We did business together.   So -
>   Tell me - who were they talking about?

And still THE SPIRIT points onwards.

SCROOGE   I will follow, Spirit.

After they have journied awhile.

SCROOGE   Not this way, Spirit.   These streets are foul and
                         dirty - every alley, every archway is a cesspit of
                         filth and grime.   And the people are no better than
                         the place.   No Spirit, not this way -

*And a DRUNK reels past them, not noticing them of course,
but disgusting SCROOGE, and still THE SPIRIT goes onwards
with SCROOGE following.   There is a shout, and a MAN in
the very depths of poverty and depravity and desperation
rushes past them, pursued by another intent of his life...
He catches the FIRST MAN and for a moment they fight
desperately.   The attached MAN gets away and rushes off,
still pursued...*

SCROOGE   Spirit, why do we come to this place?   *(THE SPIRIT
                         ignores him.)*   I have never before ventured to this
                         part of the city.   Turn back.   The place is filled
                         with thieves and murderers and drunks.   It is not
                         safe to be on the streets - please, Spirit, wait.

*The SPIRIT stops and turns and looks at SCROOGE, but does
not speak nor make any effort to turn back.*

SCROOGE   Spirit, if your purpose is to fill me with dread and
                         fear of the future, then you have succeeded.   Do
                         you mean that this is what my own life will come to?
                         That the day approaches when I shall lose - all I
                         have, and be reduced to living, to existing in a
                         place that is so filthy and horrible?   Among people
                         who have fallen as low as men can ever fall?   Tell
                         me Spirit, tell me.

*A filthy OLD HAG bearing a large bundle approaches them...
and almost at once she is called to by ANOTHER.*

WOMAN   Mrs. Dilber!

*MRS. DILBER stops and waits for the second woman to catch
her up.*

WOMAN   Well - Mrs. Dilber!   Fancy seeing you.

MRS DILBER   I might say the same about you.

WOMAN   Going to Joe's?

MRS DILBER   Where else?

WOMAN   Where else indeed?   There's not a better beetling
                  shop in the city.   *(Taking in MRS DILBER's BUNDLE -
                  similar to the one she has herself.)*   Oh, Mrs Dilber,
                  don't tell me you've been to - to HIM too?

MRS DILBER   Why not?   He was dead, wasn't he?

WOMAN   Scarcely cold, though.   Least he wasn't when I was
                  there, and by all the signs you beat me to it.

MRS DILBER   Never mind the signs, dearie;   he was dead I tell
                  you, dead as a door-nail.   *(Calling.)*   Joe!   Joe!
                  (To OTHER WOMAN.)   Come in the back ways.   He'll
                  be there all right.

WOMAN   Oh, he'll be there - expecting us too, I shouldn't
                  wonder.   *(Calling.)*   Joe!

*And as they go a crack of light comes from JOE's and we
hear him say..."Oh, it's you, Mrs. Dilber.   I wondered
who'd be first."   THE WOMEN laugh at this, and just before
the door closes another MAN comes hurrying past SCROOGE and
THE SPIRIT, calling:*

MAN   Wait, Joe.   Wait for me then.

JOE   *(Off.)* And another of you.   Why, it's the undertaker!
                  You don't waste much time do you.

*And THE MAN and THE TWO WOMEN are swallowed up in the
darkness of Joe's shop, leaving SCROOGE alone again with
THE SPIRIT.*

SCROOGE   Who are they, Spirit?   What do they mean to me?
                  And what have they in those bundles?   Is it something
                  they've stolen?

THE SPIRIT does not answer but moves towards the shop.

SCROOGE   Not in there, Spirit.   No, I couldn't bear it.   I've
                  never been to such a place in the whole of my life.
                  No, Spirit, no.   I couldn't bear the stench and the
                  filth.   Every article is decaying with dirt and
                  grease, no, no.

*But THE SPIRIT goes on.   The light changes and as it does so,
JOE comes back with his THREE VISITORS.   JOE is a seventy
year old rascal.*

JOE   Come into the parlour then, and bring yer stuff with
                  you.   I've locked up the shop so we shan't be
                  disturbed.

MRS DILBER
Don't you never sell nothing, Joe. Every time I come, there's the same stinking old rags all over the shop and the same rusty old nails and iron and filthy bones. Piles of filthy old bones.

WOMAN
He hoards them.

MRS. DILBER
I reckons you'll not be able to get out the place one day.

JOE
And what's it matter to you what I sells as long as I buys, eh, Mrs. Dilber?

THE MAN
That's what I was going to say. Will yer buy this lot, Joe?

MRS DILBER
Trust the undertaker to get us down to business.

THE MAN
And trust the charwoman to get there first.

MRS. DILBER
And if I did?

JOE
The charwoman, the laundress and the undertaker. What is it - a conspiracy?

WOMAN
Chance, Joe, pure chance. Strike me if we haven't all three met here without meaning it.

JOE
You couldn't have met in a better place. Ooooooh, me bones. Aw, you talk about the old bones in the shop. There's none here as old as mine, I can tell you. Well, what have you got? What have you got me darlins; let's see it then...

MRS. DILBER
Yes, just what have we got? Eh?

WOMAN
You can ask, Mrs. Dilber. And it's no good your looking at me like that, I'm entitled to what I can get.

MRS DILBER
Who said otherwise?

WOMAN
Every person's got a right to take care of themselves.

MRS DILBER
All right, I never said...

WOMAN
He always did, so why shouldn't I?

MRS. DILBER
All right, all right, all right, all right.

WOMAN
All right. Then don't stand there staring at me as though I've got something I'm not entitled to. Who'd be the wiser anyway? And who's going to miss them

anyway...A dead man?   D'you suppose he's going to miss them?   Eh?

And MRS DILBER laughs and breaks the tension.

MRS DILBER   No, no, I reckon he's not.

WOMAN   And if he did want 'em after he's dead, why didn't he do like everybody else and have someone to look after him when he was ill.   Mean old screw.   Lying there, gasping out his last, all on his own.   I tell you it wasn't natural.

MRS DILBER   Ah, it was a judgement on him.

WOMAN   Well, it wasn't heavy enough judgement.   I tell you' it'd been heavier still if I could have laid my hands on anything else.

THE MAN   Well, here's my lot, Joe.   What's that worth to you?

JOE   *(Studying the articles THE UNDERTAKER has put in front of him.)* A couple of seals, a pencil-case, what's this?   Pair of sleeve buttons...and a brooch.

THE MAN   That's worth something, Joe.

JOE   No, it's not.   It's hardly worth nothing.

THE MAN   Ah, but Joe...

JOE   Five bob, the lot.

THE MAN   Five bob?

JOE   Take it or leave it, it's all the same to me.   I wouldn't give you another six pence for that lot if you was to boil me alive.   Who's next?

MRS DILBER   I'm next.   Here, have a look at this lot.   *(Untying her bundle.)* Here - sheets and towels.

JOE   There's not much in those.

MRS DILBER   Some old clothes.

JOE   They're old all right.   I'll grant you that.   Worn them all his life I shouldn't wonder.

MRS DILBER   Yeah, but have a look at this pair of spoons, Joe. Real silver they are.   And so's these sugar tongs.

JOE	Real silver, yeat.
THE MAN	Don't go ruining yourself over that lot, Joe.
JOE	I always did ruin myself over the ladies; it's a weakness of mine. I always gives 'em too much.
WOMAN	Too much! Huh!
JOE	Five and ninepence.
MRS DILBER	What!
JOE	Not another penny. And if yer haggles with me I'll knock half a crown of it.
MRS DILBER	I'd get double that anywhere else.
JOE	Then take it somewhere else.
WOMAN	Now open up my bundle, Joe. *(He starts doing so.)*
MRS DILBER	Five and ninepence. Ain't worth the journey getting 'ere, let alone all the trouble I was put to.
JOE	*(To woman.)* What yer got in here then?
WOMAN	It'll keep till you opens it.

JOE gets it open.

JOE	What d'you call this, then?
WOMAN	Have a good look Joe. You'll know.
JOE	Bed curtains?
WOMAN	*(laughing.)* I said you'd know. Yeah, bed curtains.
JOE	You don't mean to say you took em down, rings an' all, with him lying there?
WOMAN	And why not?
JOE	You were born to make your fortune.
MRS DILBER	And she'll do it too.
WOMAN	D'you expect me to resist the chance for the likes of him?
JOE	*(Still with the bundle.)* And are these his blankets?

WOMAN   Who elses?

JOE   I hope he didn't die of anything catching? Eh?

WOMAN   Don't be afraid of that, Joe. D'you suppose I was
                so fond of him that I'd hang around for stuff like
                that if he had.

JOE   Lor, love us - is this his shirt?

*With general exclamations of astonishment, the three crowd
round.*

WOMAN   Aye, and his finest one too.   You won't find a hole
                in it anywhere.

MRS DILBER   That didn't belong to him.

WOMAN   Oh, yes it did.

MRS DILBER   How come I didn't see it then?

WOMAN   Perhaps you didn't look at him properley.

JOE   Look at him! You mean...

WOMAN   They'd have wasted it if it hadn't been for me.

JOE   What d'you call wasting of it?

WOMAN   They'd have buried him in it.   Some fool had put it
                on him already.

MRS DILBER   And you took it off?

WOMAN   And why not?. Isn't calico good enough to be buried
                in?   He couldn't look any uglier in calico than he
                looked in that.

JOE   Make your fortune you will.

WOMAN   What else could he have expected.   He frightened
                everyone away from him when he was alive - just to
                profit us when he was dead.

*They all laugh in their hideous glee and JOE starts to hand
money to them all through the laughter, as the light fades
from the scene...*

SCROOGE   (*To SPIRIT.*) Spirit, I begin to understand.   You are
                showing me what has happened to some poor, unhappy man
                as a warning of what might happen to me.   Is that it,
                Spirit.   This man, whoever he was,   lived rather as

I do now - and I, I could come to the same terrible
end.   Tell me if that is so, spirit.

Still THE SPIRIT does not answer.

Spirit, I shall not lose by this lesson. But Spirit,
someone in this town must have felt something for
this man's death.   Show me such a person.   Show me.

*THE SPIRIT turns and points, and light comes up on a YOUNG
WOMAN, holding her baby in her arms, pacing up and down
waiting.   Soon she hears footsteps hurring towards her and
moves quickly to HER HUSBAND as he arrives.*

HUSBAND   Caroline, you shouldn't have waited up.

CAROLINE   I had to know.   Well? *(He doesn't answer.)* Is it
                   good or bad?

HUSBAND   Bad.

CAROLINE   Then we are completely ruined.

HUSBAND   Not completely.   There's a faint hope.

CAROLINE   But we owe him money.   He'll demand every penny, and
                   he won't give us any more time to pay.   You don't
                   imagine he'll relent do you.

HUSBAND   He's past relenting, Caroline.   He's dead.

CAROLINE   Thank God. No - I'm sorry.   I shouldn't have said
                   that.

HUSBAND   You remember when I went to see him last night they
                   told me he was ill.   I thought it was just an
                   excuse.   Apparently he was not only ill, but dying
                   even then.

CAROLINE   And who will they transfer our debt to now?

HUSBAND   I don't know Caroline.   That's what I mean by a
                   faint hope.   We might be able to raise the money
                   before they transfer it to anyone.

CAROLINE   Whoever it is, they can't possibly be as mean and
                   unkind as he was.   No one could treat us as badly
                   as that.

*And as the scene fades swiftly from view SCROOGE turns
desperately to THE SPIRIT.*

SCROOGE Spirit, please do not torture me any more.   Show
me one person - surely there must be one - who feels
tenderness about the death of another.   Show me
some moment of tenderness or I shall be haunted by
these sights for ever.

THE SPIRIT does not answer but leads SCROOGE away.

SCROOGE Oh, Spirit, I am thankful to leave this place and to
be again among streets and sights I know.   Lead on.
Lead on, Spirit.

And THE SPIRIT takes him farther onwards...and stops.

SCROOGE I know this street.   I know the house.   Why,
Spirit...

*But before he can speak any more, light comes up on the
CRATCHIT household.*
Mrs Cratchit
Martha Cratchit
Belinda Cratchit
Peter Cratchit
*But Bob Cratchit is not present...and Tiny Tim's special
corner is empty, his stool is there; so, too, is his crutch.*

ALL are sitting very still and quiet.   PETER is reading.

PETER C. "And he took a child, and set him in the midst of them".

*And there is silence and stillness, and then MRS CRATCHIT
and THEIR DAUGHTERS continue with sewing, and PETER just sits.
After a while MRS CRATCHIT puts down her sewing, and puts
her hand up to her face.*

MARTHA Mother?

MRS CRATCHIT It's the sewing.   The colour hurts my eyes.   I'll
be all right in a moment.

MARTHA You're doing too much.

MRS CRATCHIT No.   There - they're all right again now.   I think
it's the candle-light that makes them weak.   Don't
mention anything to your father, will you.

MARTHA Are you sure you're all right?

MRS CRATCHIT Yes, of course.   I don't want your father to know.
He has enough to worry him without my silly old eyes.

BELINDA Father ought to be home by now.   It's near his time.

PETER Past it.   But father walks slower than he used to.

MRS CRATCHIT	Bless him *(A long pause.)* I've known him walk so fast, even with....even with Tiny Tim on his shoulder.

And they all remember this and say so...almost in chorus.

MRS CRATCHIT	But he was very light to carry, and his father loved him so much that it was never any trouble.
MARTHA	There's father now.
MRS CRATCHIT	Please.

She goes to meet and greet him, and the other members of the family are all to ready to bring him by the fire, to fuss him, to comfort him, and yet hardly a word is said by the mouth, the eyes and the touch are always sufficient. Eventually he is settled...

MRS CRATCHIT	Did you go today, Robert?
BOB	Yes, my dear. I wish you could have gone. It would have done you good to see how green a place it is. But you'll see it often. I promised him we would go there every Sunday. Oh, Tiny Tim, Tiny Tim, *(For a moment he breaks down, and again the silent unity of the family is there. After a moment or two, in which MRS CRATCHIT is the only person to make the outward sign of comfort...he tries to pull himself together.)*
BOB	I must tell you. I met Mr Scrooge's nephew today.
MRS CRATCHIT	Fred?
BOB	He was so kind. He stopped me in the street and said that I seemed to be just a little down, not quite my usual self.
MRS CRATCHIT	Did you tell him, Robert?
BOB	Yes, my dear, I told him. I told him. He really is the kindest gentleman. The pleasantest spoken gentleman you ever heard. He said "I'm heartily sorry for it, Mr Cratchit", and then he said "and I'm heartily sorry for your good wife". By-the-bye, how he ever knew THAT I don't know.
MRS CRATCHIT	Knew what, me dear?
BOB	That you were a good wife.
PETER	Everybody knows that, father.
BOB	Yes, yes, Peter, boy, I'm sure they do.

MRS CRATCHIT   Go on with you. Both of you. What else did he say,
                 Robert?

BOB   He said I'm heartily sorry for your good wife.   Oh,
                 yes. And then he said if there was anything he could
                 do for us - and he handed me this; his card - and
                 said that that was where he lived, and that I should
                 call at any time.

MRS CRATCHIT   That was kind of him.

BOB   He meant it too. I know that. And yet - well, it
                 doesn't so much matter whether there is anything he
                 can do for us - it was just the way he said it. It
                 really seemed as if he had known our Tiny Tim and -
                 and really felt with us.

MRS CRATCHIT   He's a good soul.

BOB   He is a good soul. You'd know it even more if you
                 saw him and spoke to him. I shan't be a bit
                 surprised if he gets Peter a better job.

MRS CRATCHIT   Well, Peter. Did you hear that?

MARTHA   That's wonderful. Before we know where we are Peter
                 will be setting up partnership with someone else.

PETER   Oh, not for a long time yet.

BOB   Maybe not, but it's possible; you will eventually,
                 one of these days.

PETER   Maybe, father.

BOB   Still, there's plenty of time for that, plenty of
                 time.

*And for a long while they remain silent, then BOB speaks
again.*

BOB   Well, however and whenever we part from one another,
                 I'm sure we'll none of us forget poor Tiny Tim, shall
                 we? Nor shall we forget this first of all partings
                 among us.

*Again the support, the almost choral agreement of a family
so closely knitted together.*

BOB   And I know - I know, my dears, that when we remember
                 how patient and how quiet he was - then we shall not
                 quarrel easily among ourselves, and risk forgetting
                 little Tiny Tim.

Again the simplicity of the family agreement...

BOB
I am very happy. So very, very happy.

*And MRS CRATCHIT puts her arms around him and kisses him.
PETER comes to him and shakes his hands, and BELINDA and
MARTHA hold each others hand.   All their eyes turn to the
corner, to the empty stool and the useless crutch.   The
light fades slowly away leaving SCROOGE with the SPIRIT OF
CHRISTMAS YET TO COME.   For a long timeSCROOGE has nothing
to say, then he turns to THE GHOST.*

SCROOGE
Spirit, I feel the time is soon coming when we must
part.   Is that not so?   *(THE SPIRIT still does not
speak.)* I know it is so - I know it deep within,
Spirit, before we part, tell me - who was the man who
died, the man I heard them talking of, the man who's
clothes they sold, the man who...

*But before he can continue, THE SPIRIT turns and starts to
lead SCROOGE somewhere else, and SCROOGE follows.*

SCROOGE
Lead on, Spirit.   I will follow.   *(They journey on,
SCROOGE looking carefully at all they pass, and soon
he becomes alarmed.)* But Spirit, this way lies the
churchyard, we have passed all the places I have
known.....No!   Why in here?   Why, here in the
churchyard?

*But THE SPIRIT ignores his growing panic...which is now
again accompanied by the growing sound of a tolling
funeral bell, and leads him onwards and onwards.   Suddenly
it stops.   Pointing downwards to a particular grave,
SCROOGE looks at it, looks at the SPIRIT, suddenly the bell
sound stops...*

SCROOGE
Before I read the name that is written on this stone,
you must answer me one question.   The things that I
have seen - are they the shadows of things that WILL
BE or are they the shadows of things that only MIGHT
BE?

But THE SPIRIT stands motionless, pointing at the grave...

SCROOGE
Will you not answer me?   *(Still no answer.)* The
courses men follow will of certainty lead to a
particular ends - unless those courses change.   I
understand that, Spirit. But I also hope, I hope,
from what you have taught me, that if the courses are
changed the ends will change.   Please tell me this
is so.   Please tell me that I do not hope in vain.
Please Spirit.

But still THE SPIRIT is immovable, says nothing, and continues to point at the grave. SCROOGE turns and sweeps away the dust and leaves, then reads.

SCROOGE
"Ebenezer Scrooge. Ebenezer Scrooge." *(He turns desperately again to THE SPIRIT.)* No, Spirit, no, no. Hear me, spirit. I am not the man I was. I will not be that same man again. Why do you show me this, if I am past all hope? Oh, good Spirit, help me. Pity me. Tell me that I may yet change these shadows by changing the way I live. I will honour Christmas in my heart, and I will try to keep it all the year. I will live in the Past, the Present and the Future - the spirits of all three shall strive within me. Tell me, spirit, tell me - tell me there is yet hope...

He grasps towards THE SPIRIT's outstretched hand in an action of prayer and humility. His eyes closed, his head slowly bowing until it almost touches the ground. And THE SPIRIT moves silently away from him, watching him all the time, and when he opens his eyes he is alone.

(Author's note: If there is to be a four-poster bed, then Scrooge first clutches at the Spirit's outstretched hand, but finds himself eventually clutching one of the posts at the foot of his bed.)

He is alone in the silence.

SCROOGE
I will live in the Past, the Present and the Future. The Spirits of all three shall strive within me. O Jacob Marley! Heaven and Christmas Time be praised for this! I say it on my knees old Jacob; on my knees!

And now he opens his eyes and looks around, he is astonished to find that all is as it was.

SCROOGE
But everything is still here. Here as it was. And I am here. I am here. The shadows of the things that would have been might still be changed. They will be. I know they will be.

And now he stands, feeling and enjoying the feeling of the differences within himself.

I'm as light as a feather, I'm as happy as an angel, I'm as merry as a school-boy...I'm as giddy as a drunken man. A merry Christmas to everybody! A Happy New Year to all the world.

And he frisks about his room in growing excitement and delight.

That's where the ghost of Jacob Marley came in.
That's where the Ghost of Christmas Present sat...
Oooh, it's all right, it's all true, it's all
happened.

*And suddenly he laughs, laughs as he can never remember
having laughed before..."The father of a long long line of
brilliant laughs".*

I don't know what day of the months it is, I don't
know how long I've been among the spirits. I don't
know anything. I'm like a baby. Never mind. I
don't care. I'd rather be a baby...

*And again he whoops and hails his new found enjoyment of
life, and suddenly all the church bells let out the most
glorious and festive and celebratory sound that ever
happened, for a moment he listens, spellbound and astonished,
and he wonders...*

This is extraordinary. Why can they all be ringing
out so gloriously now? Why? Why now?

And he goes to the door (or the window.) and looks out.

But how beautiful. Beautiful..no mist, no fog.
Just the beautiful air - crisp and bright and cold
and clear. And the sunlight... and the blue of the
sky...its glorious, glorious. And the bells are
wonderful, heavenly.

He sees A LAD crossing the street and calls to him.

Hello. I say - what's today?

THE BOY   What?

SCROOGE   What's today, my fine fellow?

THE BOY   Today! Why, it's CHRISTMAS DAY.

SCROOGE   *(To himself.)* It's Christmas Day. I haven't missed
                 it. I haven't missed it. The spirits have done it
                 all in one night. Well, of course they have. They
                 can do anything they like. Of course they can. Of
                 course they can. *(To the BOY.)* Hello, my fine
                 fellow!

THE BOY   Hello!

SCROOGE   Do you know the poulterers in the next street but one,
                 at the corner?

THE BOY   I should hope I did.

SCROOGE   An intelligent boy!   A remarkable boy! Do you know
                 whether they've sold the prize turkey that was
                 hanging up in the window? - Not the little prize
                 turkey; the big one?

THE BOY   What! The one as big as me?

SCROOGE   What a delighful boy.   It's a pleasure to talk to
                 him.   Yes, my boy, that's the one.

THE BOY   It's hanging there now!

SCROOGE   It is?   Then go and buy it.

THE BOY   What!

SCROOGE   No, no, I am in earnest.   Go and buy it, and tell
                 them to bring it back here so that I can give them
                 directions where to take it.   Come back with the man -
                 and I'll give you a shilling.   Come back in less
                 than five minutes - and I'll give you a crown.

THE BOY   Yes, sir.

*And THE BOY is off like a shot, leaving a delighted and
dancing SCROOGE who laughs again and then turns to us...*

SCROOGE   I'll send it to Bob Cratchit's - and he shan't know
                 who sent it. *(Laughs.)*   It's twice the size of
                 Tiny Tim.   Oh-ho, no one ever made such a joke as
                 sending that to Bob Cratchit's will be. *(He writes
                 the address down.)* And there are shouts of "Sir!
                 Sir!   I've brought it myself sir!" - and the BOY
                 returns with the most enormous turkey.*

SCROOGE   Gracious, boy.   You can't possibly carry that to
                 Camden Town.   You must have a cab.   Here, my lad,
                 here's money for the cab...here's the address to
                 take it to...and here's the five shillings I
                 promised you.   Quickly now my lad...and a Merry
                 Christmas to you.

THE BOY   And a Merry Christmas to you too, sir.

*And again SCROOGE chuckles as he tidies himself up and
sings and dances and mutters to himself..*

SCROOGE   Of course they can.   They've done it all in one
                 night - just so I shan't miss Christmas...and bless
                 them for it.   Now, wait a minute.   What am I going
                 to do?   I know. I'll go to Fred. He's always
                 asking me - so I'll go and surprise him.

And again he laughs and off he goes towards his NEWPHEWS,
(saying "a Merry Christmas" to anyone he happens to pass)
And suddenly he sees the two PORTLY GENTLEMEN.

SCROOGE

My dear gentlemen, how nice to see you. How do you
do. I do hope you succeeded yesterday. It was
most kind of you. A Merry Christmas to you
gentlemen.

THE GENTLEMEN look at SCROOGE and then at each other and
then, quite non-plussed, simply mutter together.

BOTH GENTS

Mr Scrooge!

SCROOGE

Yes, yes, that is my name, and I fear it may not be
very pleasant to you. Allow me to ask your pardon.
And will you have the goodness to put me down for...

And he draws their heads together and whispers to them,
and to their total astonishment...

1st GENT

Lord bless me! My dear Mr Scrooge, are you serious?

SCROOGE

If you please, not a farthing less. A great many
back payments are included in it, I can assure you.
Will you do me that favour?

2nd GENT

My dear sir, I don't know what to say.

SCROOGE

Then don't say anything. Just come and see me.
Will you please come and see me.

BOTH GENTS

We will. We will.

SCROOGE

Thank'ee I thank'ee fifty times. Bless you both.

And the two men go and SCROOGE goes and calls after them...

SCROOGE

A merry Christmas to you, gentlemen, and the happiest
of New Years.

THE GENTS

(Calling back.) And to you, Mr Scrooge.

And THE MEN go off one way and SCROOGE another, and as they
go there is a sudden burst of laughter and general
merriment, and we are back in FRED's house. Rather as we
were in the party we saw with the Ghost of Christmas
Present. There are present:
Fred, his Nephew
Fred's wife

His wife's pretty sister
His wife's plain sister
His friend, Topper

FRED is again the cause of the merriment, telling them a
story.

FRED   He did.   As I'm alive, I swear he did.   He said
            Christmas was a humbug. *(More laughter.)* And you
            know what's more?   He believed it, too.   *(Yet more*
            laughter.)

F'S WIFE   The more shame on him, Fred.

FRED   He's a comical fellow, and that's the truth.

TOPPER   Comical?

FRED   Oh, he may not be all that pleasant, but he suffers
            for it more than we do.

F'S WIFE   I tell you I've no patience with him.

FRED   Oh, I have.   I'm sorry for him.   I couldn't be
            angry with him if I tried.   Well, who suffers most
            from his nasty whims?   He himself.   Nobody else.
            Here, he takes it into his head to dislike us, and
            he won't come and dine with us.   What's the
            consequence?   He doesn't lose much of a dinner...

There are howls of laughter and many protests, and during
this SCROOGE has come quite unseen into their midst, and as
the laughter reaches a certain point he says...

SCROOGE   I let myself in.   I hope you don't mind.

FRED   Why bless my soul, who's that?

SCROOGE   It's me.   Your uncle Scrooge.

There is a long silence while they all stare at SCROOGE.
And it is SCROOGE who breaks the silence.

SCROOGE   I have come to dinner.   If you'll have me.

Again a pause, then suddenly all delight breaks loose as,
led by his NEPHEW, they all make him joyously and gaily
welcome.   Suddenly all the gaiety cuts out, leaving
everyone, as it were in a moment of stillness, a still
photograph, everyone except SCROOGE and his NEPHEW...

SCROOGE   Fred will you help me tomorrow?

FRED   Help you uncle?   Of course, but how in particular?

SCROOGE

I want to play a joke - a joke on Bob Cratchit.   I want you to...

And as he whispers in FRED's ear, the party comes back to life and we do not catch what it is the joke is to be. But the lights slowly fade, as does the sound of the gaiety.

And when light comes back it is on SCROOGE arriving at his office the next morning. He turns and motions someone or something to keep out of sight, and he chuckles to himself at the thought of his joke...

SCROOGE

(To us.)   Huh! Bob Cratchit's late.   I thought he might be.   I'll play a trick on him.   He thinks I'm still the same person as I was before Christmas.   I'll pretend I am!   *(He chuckles again.)* Look out. Here he comes.

And suddenly he hears BOB CRATCHIT approaching and quickly settles to his own place of work, resuming, as far as he can recall it, his old demeanor, BOB CRATCHIT approaches and tries to slip into the office unnoticed.

SCROOGE

And what do you mean by arriving at this time of day!

BOB

I'm very sorry, sir.   I am a little late.

SCROOGE

You are.   Yes, I think you are.   Step this way, sir, if you please.

BOB

(Approaching him.) It's only once a year, sir.

SCROOGE

Only once a year...

BOB

I promise it won't happen again.   I was making rather merry yesterday, sir.

SCROOGE

Oh, you were, were you.   Well, I'll tell you what my friend.   I am not going to stand this sort of thing much longer.   In fact - I'm not going to stand it any longer.   And therefore - therefore - I'm about to raise your salary, Bob.   A merry Christmas, Bob.   A merrier Christmas Bob, my good fellow, than I have ever given you for many a year.   I shall raise your salary; I shall try to help you and your family, and we shall discuss your affairs this very afternoon over a Christmas bowl of steaming punch.   And Bob, look. Look...

And FRED arrives with HIS WIFE, and there is MRS CRATCIT and TINY TIM, and there is TOPPER and the TWO CRATCHIT DAUGHTERS, and PETER CRATCHIT, and there is joy and dancing and gaiety in abundance.   And a merry Christmas for all of us, including the audience.

EPILOGUE

BOB CRATCHIT

Scrooge was better than his word. He did it all, and even more. And to Tiny Tim he was a second father. He became as good a friend, as good a master, and as good a man as the good old city knew, or any other good old city, town, or borough in the good old world. Some people laughed to see the alteration in him, but he let them laugh and took no notice of them; for he was wise enough to know that nothing ever happened on this globe - for good - without some people having their fill of laughter at it. His own heart laughed, and that was quite enough for him. And for ever afterwards, it was always said of him that he knew how to keep Christmas well - as well as any man has ever kept it. May that be truly said of us, and all of us. And so, as Tiny observed, God bless us, Every One.

THE END.

9 780874 409024